THE HAPPY COUNTRYMAN

THE
HAPPY
COUNTRYMAN

H.E. Bates

Illustrated by C.F. Tunnicliffe

R

ROBINSON PUBLISHING
LONDON

Robinson Publishing
11 Shepherd House
5 Shepherd Street
London W1Y 7LD

First published in 1943
Published by Robinson Publishing 1985
Text copyright © The Estate of H.E. Bates
Illustrations © The Estate of C.F. Tunnicliffe

Bates, H.E.
The happy countryman.
1. Country life —— England   2. England ——
Social life and customs —— 20th century
I. Title
942.084'092'4   S522.G7
ISBN 0-948164–23–9

Printed in England by Richard Clay (The Chaucer Press) Ltd.

Contents

Full-Page Illustrations

I

Et Decorum Est Pro Patria Mori

THERE is a road in the West Sussex hills that runs between mixed woodland and fields of barley. On summer evenings, during war at any rate, there is hardly ever anyone on it except a soldier or an airman with his girl, and there are few sounds on the hillside except the sounds of birds and the distant chatter, coming from the south, of a Hurricane testing its cannon over the sea. This road is like countless other English roads in the south: primroses about the oak roots in spring, scabious edging the tender green barley in July; wind in the high beeches, stillness in the steep gulleys of the road below. It was never a busy road, even in peace-time, except for one week of the year, when cars and buses and, in another age, brakes and wagonettes, went up the hill for the fashionable summer race meetings on the downs. There are no race meetings now, no cars or wagonettes, no brakes or buses. There are no streaming crowds, no roadside touts. There are no placards asking you to patronise somebody's beer, somebody's ice-cream, or the old firm. All you can read now is an incomplete inscription scratched by someone on a

7

gate in the woodland. It looks as if it might have been scratched with a nail, perhaps by an airman or a soldier in an idle moment, and it is already so faint that after a few months of winter rain it will probably be washed away. " Et decorum est," it reads, " pro patria mori."

This is not the only inscription. Ten yards farther on there is another. It is printed and nailed securely on a piece of board so that it will not blow away. It has an air of genteel restraint about it. " The public is reminded that this is private property. Trespassers will be prosecuted."

I stood for a long time on an evening in the third summer of the war looking at these inscriptions, thinking about them. After a time I went back to the Georgian mansion which was the Mess of a number of young officers who might also at any moment die for their country, and I thought of them again. Some hours later I went to bed in the oak-panelled room, with its white plaster frieze of animals and birds, which was the bedroom I shared with an observer, an Australian and a dentist, and I thought of them again. The room in which I slept, expensively panelled, charmingly decorated, with its leaded terrace of Portland stone looking out on vistas of acacia and rhododendron and avenues of giant limes and chestnuts, seemed to belong to the world of one inscription—the public is reminded that this is private property. The men with whom I shared it, and the men who shared the house above and below and about me, seemed to belong to the other—et decorum est pro patria mori. The house, and not only the house but the time, and not only the time but perhaps the very moment, seemed to be the meeting place of two worlds, or if not two worlds at least two ways of life. There is a poem by Hardy called " At the Time of the Breaking of Nations," and here, somewhere between the idly scratched inscription that might also have been scratched on wood in the same place by a Roman legionary two thousand years ago, and the reminder that a piece of Sussex earth was private property, it seemed possible that a nation was being broken up. Not broken down. But broken up: to be re-smelted, re-moulded and, one hoped, re-dedicated to something like the simple nobility of the Latin inscription scratched on a gate by a field of barley.

Is it right to die for one's country? Is it right that there should be private property? Is it necessary to answer? Whether we like it or not there is an impact of ideals. Whether we like it or not the questions have to be answered.

It is curious that the answers are not very simple. If it is right to die for one's country, then it is rather a disconcerting fact that the English countryside shows no sign of having flowered profusely on the

. . . under a big magnolia tree there was
a deep hole made by a fallen Heinkel.

9

blood of heroes. If it is wrong, as we so often argue, that there should be private property, then it is curious that practically nine-tenths of the English countryside has flowered into its special beauty under the benefits of private ownership. The downs above the road where the inscription is scratched on the gate are among the loveliest hills in England. They were there when the Romans came: wild, solitary, washed white by rain. Today their beauty is the beauty of private ownership, of a great house, of an expensive way of life, now dead, which was vital and magnificent enough to survive every social and economic change until our time.

There have been times in my life when, having been born in a little house, I have wanted to live in a large one. Now at last I have lived in one for a whole summer. On a day when the winter was breaking up I drove my car from the east side of Kent to the west side of Sussex and found myself, that evening, billeted in a mansion that was probably built in the hungry forties of the last century. In Kent it was snowing, but in East Sussex, on the bone-bare hills about Lewes, the snow was no thicker than chalk dust, and in West Sussex, under the ridge of downs and close to the sea, there was no snow at all. The mansion stood yellow and bare and cold in its garden of magnificent trees. Some of its windows had been blown out and repaired again with glass substitute. Under the huge portico of the front doorway the plaster had been shattered away. In the garden, under a big magnolia tree turned coffee brown by frost, there was a deep hole made by a fallen Heinkel. The hungry forties—the destructive forties. After a hundred years the broken windows, the shattered plaster and the defiled garden were more than symbolic. The age that built the house was dead; the age that did not build the house was breaking it down.

The most frequent comment on that house during that summer was on its impossibility. It was a square stucco house in late Georgian style with a stone terrace on the south and west sides. It looked over a garden of three or four acres, and beyond that were its own meadows of eight or ten acres carefully bordered by evergreen trees. Beyond that, to the north-east, were the hills, and to the south-west the sea. Behind the house, to the north, were the stables, and to the side of them the kitchen gardens walled with ten-feet walls under which, on the south side, were the glass-houses. The peaches and pears on those walls were past their best, but the currant trees were ten feet high. Farther beyond the gardens was a paddock of two acres or so, and beyond that, under a belt of trees, what must have passed in Victorian times for a rock garden, carefully placed so that no one could see it.

Out of sight of the house were the cottages. The stables were if anything rather better built and better looking than the cottages, but if you belonged to the outside world beyond the thick shelter of evergreen, oaks and hollies and yews and laurustinus, you could not see either of them anyway.

Here, in fact, someone had built a self-contained world. If you made an attempt to look at it without prejudice—difficult enough when your life was bound up with Spitfires and Beaufighters and friends who were with you at lunch but did not return for tea—you were forced to admit that it represented the completest unit in our rural history. It was a world of beauty, usefulness, employment, security. The house had been built with pride and style; the trees, chosen from many parts of the world, had been planted with intelligence and artistry. Cows had given milk and beef; horses had given exercise and pleasure and, of course, manure. In the paddock there had been saddle of mutton and spring leg of lamb; there was pork in the orchard. In the gardens, under the walls and the glass, you had all the fruit you wanted: peaches and pears, cherries and apricots, grapes and cucumbers. Big shaggy yellow and gold and white chrysanthemums came into the house at Christmas with the holly from the shrubberies and the pheasants from the spinneys. In winter the dance in drawing-rooms, in summer the flower show under the acacia trees—was there anything else to ask?

A century later, to a hundred and fifty officers concerned largely with the business of shooting down the enemy before he shot down them, that world naturally seemed impossible and unreal. The social order was upside down. The big, beautifully panelled rooms, once inviolate, were noisy with officers playing shove ha'penny and invaded by W.A.A.F.s serving beer and coffee. The billiard room, once the prerogative of gentlemen in starched shirts smoking cigars, had been invaded by young men from New Zealand and Australia, Canada and South Africa, France and Holland and Poland and Czecho-Slovakia, playing hilarious and blasphemous games of snooker. In other ages the echo of war was already very soft before it reached the inner heart of this insulated rural world. Now the house was of the war; the blast of war had even broken its windows. No part of it was inviolate any longer. From being a secure, private, self-contained, self-insulated unit into which not even the whisper of a social disturbance, let alone a world disturbance, need enter, it had become the equivalent of a command headquarters in the front line.

What impressed me all that spring and summer was not the impossibility of that house but its beauty. I could not help being impressed even by its outworn perfection. Every principle I held was

11

against a rural life governed by privilege; I hoped we should never see in England again a social system of two classes. Yet as I looked at this house, impossible to us, perfect of its age and kind, impressing its expansive beauty on a considerable radius of countryside, I had to ask myself if we had anything to put in its place. If you looked at it dispassionately it was an entirely selfish world. But if you looked at most other economic developments through the nineteenth century, they too were selfish. The colossal materialism of nineteenth-century progress, culminating in successive wars, had left us as the most obvious of its legacies some of the most hideous towns, notably London south of the Thames, in the world. Practically all urban expansion during the last hundred years, in places where money was to be made, has been selfish. It survives as a monstrous, planless, æsthetically meaningless expression of the times in which it was undertaken.

Could we say the same of the great house? Its selfishness too was monstrous. To fence in a piece of the world, to barricade it with trees, plant it with luxurious fruits, inhabit it with expensive horseflesh, fat cattle and exotic birds, to make the scene inside beautiful and serene and satisfactory to contemplate and not to trouble very much about the state of things outside, to confine your friends to one specified social stratum and those who kept you in comfort to another, to demand and receive service and subservience, to put the value of your horses in thousands of pounds and the value of your servants at twenty pounds a year—could it be more selfish? Yet the major legacy of this way of life was not, as with other material developments during the time, ugliness, but great beauty. And as long as the social structure remained as it was, in two layers, of two classes, the beauty could remain, constant and enviable and fat. It simply mellowed with the years.

But now the Heinkel falls by the magnolia tree. The privilege that kept the horses fat has gone. We have become, if we are not broken altogether in the process of trying to preserve ourselves, a middle-class nation. We do not want to work for people in great houses; fewer and fewer of us want to own great houses for people to work in. We want to be free. So the great house, with its selfish, enviable perfection, slips another stage out of our lives. One war broke its power; another destroys even its utility. It remains a splendid melancholy anachronism, and we have discovered nothing to put in its place.

The beauty of the house and its garden grew on me very much as the summer went on. Perhaps the selfishness that had erected it was very despicable; but you could learn much from the results. The pergola running beyond the large acacia tree—someone had had the delightful idea of planting it with laburnum and white and purple wistaria, instead of roses, so that in June it was like a tunnel of lemon and mauve. It needed only late clematis, flowering in July and August, to make it a perfect thing. At the end of it were great beds of azalea: apricot, pink, yellow, terra-cotta, planted above bright blue forget-me-nots. Nearer the house was a great magnolia, its flowers like large mauve-white porcelain goblets in late spring. Great limes, great Atlantic cedars, great mulberries: everything on the large scale. The rhododendrons made splendid lavish bonfires of crimson and scarlet in May and June. If you were to try to imitate nature in a garden this was the way to imitate it: largely, lavishly, spaciously. All you needed was an army of men to keep nature from reclaiming its own.

And now, unfortunately, the armies of men were engaged in other things. The established seclusion was invaded. Not only here, but all over the country, the beautiful impossibility of the great house was a ludicrous survival. Once again, have we anything to put in its place? The age that raised it may have been selfish, but like many selfish pursuits it was also creative. Our own age, which has nothing to put in its place, is essentially destructive. The smashed windows, the shattered plaster, the gaping roof, the Heinkel in the garden: none of them are simply symbolic, none of them are really accidents. They are the result of what we are. They are the destructive element of our time.

II

The Great House

AS I travelled backwards and forwards between the North Downs of Kent and the West Downs of Sussex, beginning in late winter when snow was on the hills and going on till past midsummer when the oats were already ripening between Chichester and the sea, I gradually came to the firm conviction that this was the best country in England. Sussex, like Devon, has been stupidly plugged in the beauty-spot business for the last quarter of a century; not quite so stupidly, but in rather a more refined way, though stupidly enough. Outsiders have therefore received an impression that Sussex is an arty-crafty hinterland of London, overpowered by the false antique and the mother-and-daughter tea room, and consequently despicable. There is also an impression that Sussex can no longer give any elbow room. The charm, over-plugged by bad Georgian poets, has hung chintz on every woodland and a tea-cosy on every haystack. The villages are over-developed; the country is a sideline; you cannot see the view for the people.

Travelling straight through Sussex, from one end to another, between the two great Assize towns, everything I saw created the entirely opposite impression. There is a hill beyond Cranbrook, on the west side, below which the whole of the east side of Sussex seems to lie before you. I used to reach it mostly in the early afternoons. The car would go slowly up it until there was a moment when it almost stopped on the crest and the view became for a second or two fixed before me: a great view of forty or fifty miles, almost mauve with haze on summery afternoons. The impression was then that you were looking across the roof of a forest, and since this was in fact once the heart of the great forest of Anderida the impression was not altogether wrong. The effect was that in a couple of thousand years man had succeeded in intersecting that forest with strips of pasture, white roads, belts of cornland and squares of orchard, without really destroying the continuity of the great woodland. There was another hill, halfway to Lewes, from which there was an entirely different view that gave a closer example of the same thing. The road ran sideways along this hill, giving a view of the loveliest of all Sussex country: the folded hill country spreading towards Tunbridge Wells. From here there was no mauve haze. The sun was to the side and not in the distance and the land was clean and clear as a map. But the impression of a forest broken up by pasture, farm and road, of a land underpopulated rather than overpopulated, was exactly the same. The tradition of settling the English village in a hollow, near water, and the later development of the great house, carefully sheltered by plantations of trees, has resulted in a landscape which often seems, from a distance, to contain very little habitation at all. So this sideways view of Sussex always gave an impression of untouched spaciousness. The horizon was vast and the sky seemed lifted up, never oppressive. The predominant colour was always green: the green of woods, pasture, growing crops, orchards in summer leaf. The few signs of settlement appeared to have been thrown across it casually, red and brown and blue, an afterthought on the original design.

The impression continued as far as Lewes, where the whole country is dominated by the bony line of the seaward Downs. It had hardly time to renew itself between Lewes, set rather majestically on a hill, and Brighton, set very majestically by the sea, but it continued exactly the same towards Arundel and the west. If the popular impression of Sussex as a sort of rural suburbia is wrong, then the idea of Brighton as a monstrous merry-go-round is also wrong. The day may come when Brighton will be an architectural show-place, when those who care for the intelligent phases of England's urban development will go, as indeed they should now, and contemplate very seriously not only the

15

way Regency architects planned a great sea front but the way early Victorian architects continued it towards Kemp Town. Even the Victorians did not all want to live in great houses, complete with a supporting retinue of peasants and pheasants, in the seclusion of the country. Some, quite reasonably, wanted to live in towns, and others began to discover that it was pleasant to live in a town by the sea. Some results of their discovery are seen in Brighton. The magnificence of the Regency front, the stone rich and yellow as country cream in the sea light of hot summer afternoons, is the best thing of its kind we possess outside the Royal Crescent, the London terraces and the Squares of Edinburgh. But I doubt if we possess anywhere a line of domestic architecture to equal the clean and dignified sweep on the front of Kemp Town. Its conception is not that of a single great mind, like the incomparable Royal Crescent at Bath, but is the result of many minds thinking in terms of a decent conception for a public street. Almost every house of that long line, bow-windowed boarding-house, black-and-white flint, blistered cream stucco, Palladian terrace, is in itself an individual decent conception of what a house should be, and yet is an unselfish contribution to the plan as a whole. In summer, but also on winter afternoons when the colour of English sunlight is unequalled in its amber tenderness in the world, this terrace has the most dignified and fascinating splendour.

We tend still to despise the Victorians, whose record of social indifference to children and the underdog is so horrific, and we tend still to despise towns like Brighton, popularly regarded as monstrosities by the sea. But once again, have we anything to put in the place of the things we despise? In recent years there has been a good deal of talk about a drift from the country to the town, as if it were an entirely modern phenomenon, but very little talk of the drift towards the sea. We have talked much about the despoiling of the countryside, a fact of which there were barely half a dozen examples across the whole of Sussex, but very little of the despoiling of the coast. We are an island people with a remarkable heritage of coastline and possibly the greatest sea traditions in the world. The natural beauty of that coastline is so great that it seems surprising we have produced so little literature on the subject: but not so surprising, perhaps, when we consider how little literature we have produced, as a seafaring nation, of the sea.

Do we care for the things we naturally possess? During the last forty years, still more intensely during the last quarter of a century, we have been systematically despoiling the coast of England. From the mouth of the Thames down to Devon it is as if a huge sewing machine has run an unrestricted and hideous embroidery. It is ten

The Victorians conceived a town as a town and kept it as such. We see the result in Brighton.

17

years since I saw the coastline north of the Thames, but it was then, if anything, slightly worse. We have joined up the coast towns of Kent and Sussex and Hampshire, and rather less blatantly those of Dorset and Devon, with a thin line of brick and concrete and wire. If there is any serious despoliation of the English countryside it is this: the seaside bungalow, the concrete block of flats by the sand dune, the holiday camp on the salt flats, the seaside streets of semi-detached. In a hundred years man may be presumed to have advanced a little. Have we anything better to offer than the Victorians? Anything as good? The development of the coast, whether by the Regency terraces of Brighton or the bungaloid switchback of Rottingdean, is a phenomenon of modern times. When we are accused of the planlessness of our towns we have the pat reply that they were planned centuries ago and that all our efforts at improvement have since been stultified by that fact. We have no such reply about the development of the coast.

The coast has been almost entirely developed within the last hundred and fifty years, and its development is roughly parallel with the development of the railway and the road. The Victorians and ourselves are almost wholly responsible: the Victorians for the towns, ourselves for what now lies between. To the Victorians goes the credit for adding to English life a series of seaside developments that have passed securely into tradition: the promenade and the esplanade are theirs; the boarding-house, the bandstand, the Winter Gardens, the aquarium, the pier, the formal carpets of flowers. They created the prim little façades of the sea front and the harbour, the neat bow-windowed terraces and the stucco hotels. These contributions were positive and creative. The Victorians conceived a town as a town and kept it as such. We see the result in Brighton, the charming sea front of St. Leonards, even in the grimy correctness of Dover, and in the unassuming charm of Sidmouth between its shoulders of red and emerald hills.

We have nothing to offer that can decently stand beside them. Wherever there was an empty strip of land with a sea view we have, with few exceptions, developed it. " Ripe for Development " has been the title of our work in progress. The great house in decay, the coast-line in development: both are expressions of something negative. In Romney Marsh we possess a piece of unique countryside: highly fertile, strange in atmosphere, with curious shingle beaches that run inland and merge with reeds and grass, an enchanting solitary stretch of land that seems cut off from the rest of the world. What we have done to its coastline of shingle and sand dune between Hythe and Rye will be seen better, perhaps, in the next chapter. The Downs about Brighton have long been a controversial subject. We have nothing like their bare shaven lines in the whole of England. What we have done to them where they overlook the sea can be seen by anybody who takes a three-penny bus ride eastwards out of Brighton.

Many of our ancestors kept away from the sea, except to sail on it. We have drifted towards it, so that in peace-time, at any rate, the seaside was the most popular national pastime. To the hideousness of our coastal development we have now added, inevitably, the desolation of war defences. The bombed cities hurt us to look at, but the dust at least has no form. The deserted sea front, more especially the deserted ribbons of concrete and bungalow, are haunting. Their form remains. They wait behind the barricade of steel and barbed wire. For what? To be reinhabited, reanimated, repeated in the post-war world expressive of what we feel for the sea, our national heritage?

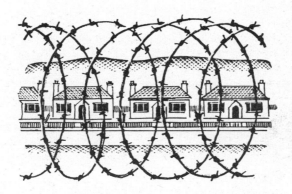

III

Sea Days, Sea Flowers

IN peace-time, if you could call it that, we used to wait for a cloud-
less morning any time from early spring to November, and then
drive down through the flat Thanet country, the Kent marshes, or
across the rolling Sussex hinterland to the sea: either eastward as far
as the white dunes of Sandwich Bay, where in winter the wind comes
straight off the ice of the Baltic, or southward to the flat wide shores
beyond the Dymchurch sea wall and the old military canal, or south-
westward to Hastings and Rye, where small Scandinavian timber ships
used to lie high on the mud slopes at low tide, unloading golden cargoes
of timber among the black wooden warehouses on the narrow quay.
Between these eastward and westward points there is a considerable
range of countryside and almost as great a range of shore. From the
upland orchard country beyond the North Downs, protected and
broken up by woods of pine and beech, you can see far off the broken
glass of the sea pools on the marshes and sometimes a flock of sails
turning in the wind on summer days; or from the south slope of the
Downs, where the bluebells are like blue hill-lakes in the break of the

beech woods and the wild strawberries are so common that you tire of gathering them on breezy, warm June afternoons, you can turn south-westward and see the smoke stacks of ships steaming up the Channel as they come in close at Dungeness and sometimes the very faint line of the horizon, without which they seem to move like shadowy toys, gliding in slow suspense between land and air. From this same point you can see the humpback line of the South Downs, forty miles away, and the Weald between. The impression is of unbroken greenness, of fields, hedgerows, woodland, with perhaps a cloud of moving smoke from a train or a wisp of stationary smoke that is an orchard in bloom in spring: the impression of a land hardly populated.

It was down through this sort of country that we used to make the coast journeys for which it was always so easy, in peace-time, to find a light excuse: the cloudlessness of the day itself, the need for change, a bathe, a walk on cliffs or shore, to wave goodbye to ships, to make sand castles, to buy fish. Down on the harbour quay at Folkestone the smacks used to lie close in under the steep walls, copper sails flagged in the shelter of the harbour, light fawn-gold nets slung out on the drying-poles in the sun, swinging like curtains, lobster pots stacked here and there on the fish-smeared flagstones or piled under the low railway arches over which the boat trains ran into the port. Whenever you went there it seemed the fish was just in. It was in the boats and they were piling it into bath tins and bringing it ashore up the steps; or it was already ashore and it lay everywhere, if it was a good catch, on the concrete floor of the market, in tins and boxes or baskets, silvery, bloody, still leaping, red-spotted plaice, halibut, dog-fish, cod, soles, mackerel, herring, oceans of silver sprats, with the gulls screaming and diving above; or the auctioneer was already selling it to a crowd that never seemed to be listening but only gazing heavily at the wet concrete where the dog-fish were still panting and leaping and the turbot looked like solid marble; or it was already sold and they were skinning the dog-fish and packing the boxes for the trains, and the old men were already baiting the lines for another trip and the hawkers already piling the fish into lumps on the barrows standing between the chandler's store and the mission hall. " Sixpence a lump, lady, where you like." You walked past and looked at all the barrows and thought of how much you paid for stale cod a hundred miles from the coast or the price of fried sole in Piccadilly. You walked past and came back and finally picked your barrow. If it was a hot, slack day, or for that matter a cold, raw day, the man had gone for a drink and somebody fetched him; he came wiping the beer off his mouth and threw a bucket of water over the white lumps of plaice and sole and halibut and flapped

21

a fish on the board. " Sixpence a lump, lady." But you knew the game and you made a wholesale deal. " How much for half a crown ?" Little plaice, sweet as nuts, would be about a penny, fat soles ninepence or a shilling, halibut big enough for a family round about two shillings. He would throw in the halibut and half a dozen plaice, or a dozen plaice and a couple of soles. You pretended it wasn't good enough and he said: " Lady, don't ruin me ! I'm gonna be married ! Don't ruin me before I start, lady !" You would pull his leg. " Married ? You're ruined already." He was a nice fellow, brown, blue-eyed, smiling, and in the end, according to him, you broke his heart. For three shillings he wrapped up the halibut and a couple of soles, or three soles and half a dozen plaice and he was quite happy. " Fillet 'em for you, lady ?" Then you broke his back. One of the children would produce a penny and speak her piece. " Judith wants a fish too," she would say, and at that he would break down. " Judith wants a fish, Judith wants a fish, Judith wants a fish ! So Judith wants a fish, does she ? Oh, hell ! give her a fish ! Do the others want one too ?" And we would say, " Yes, the others want one too," and he would say, " Oh, hell ! give them one." And at last we would come away, everyone laughing, the children each carrying their penny plaice wrapped in newspaper and all waving goodbye.

It is a long time since you could make an excursion like that. Beyond the last nets hanging to dry on the chains of the quay wall there used to be an amusement park with shooting gallery and bumpers and slot machines and a whelk-stall. On hot summer days the air was startling with the smell of sun-warmed seaweed, the fish, the whelks and the vinegar. On the stretch of dirty sand beyond the harbour hundreds of people paddled and bathed, dug in the sand, and slept. The white Channel steamers came in fast, turning to come in stern first, and coasters slipped away beyond the high white point of chalk that dazzled like snow in the sun.

From this point westward to the flat shore of Winchelsea Beach there was scarcely a mile of the coast that did not hurt the eyes. As the cliffs end and the land abruptly breaks down to the level of the marsh, the frowsy ribbon of seaside houses and huts unrolls itself. The high sea wall is broken at intervals by the old Martello towers and at last by the dunes seaward from New Romney. It is this piece of coast that is full of Napoleonic memories and of odd Napoleonic monuments, such as the Martello towers and the military canal, and which is, as in Napoleonic days, a vital line of defence against whatever may come in from the sea. The piece of country immediately behind it inspired someone to talk of " five continents and Romney Marsh." This flat,

. . . *the tall mauve-pink marshmallows, like delicate wild hollyhocks, would sway among the clusters of reed.*

23

strange sea country, of rich sheep pasture, of dykes feathered with reed, of great deserted stretches of inland shingle, would be held sometimes on hot afternoons of July and August in a lofty reflected glow of light that gave it a sense of superb remoteness. Wind would turn the willow leaves grey-white in the sun; the tall mauve-pink marshmallows, like delicate wild hollyhocks, would sway among the clusters of reed and willow-herb and purple loosestrife that marked the lines of dykes across the pastures. I have never seen these mallows elsewhere, and the taller tree-mallow, which is rare among coastal rocks in the south and west, not at all. Both may be called sea flowers; both occur only near the coasts of England and Ireland, rarely in Scotland.

The sea has on flowers something of the same effect as altitude. It rarefies them. It reduces them, like the toy passenger train that peeps and shrieks across the flat marsh from Hythe to the point at Dungeness, to a miniature level. Dune and shore and tideless stretches of shingle correspond to alpine moraine and scree, in which starvation produces delicacy. Yet there are flowers here, on the marsh shingles, which by all association do not seem to belong here. The thrift of cottage gardens, neat green pincushions stuck with hatpins whose pink heads are like everlasting flowers preserved on the slate mantelpieces of unused front rooms, seems to have no right to be called sea pink. You see it everywhere across the shingle, flowering from about mid-summer to October, when the sea gales begin to whip the skin off the land. Its prim pink flowers edge the roadside, seed across the railway track. They spring up in the cracks on the concrete paths and on the unsold lots of the new holiday towns that lie in naked concrete strips between marsh and sea. Some day someone will write about the life of these towns of one street that runs for miles parallel to the sea: the white harsh light rebounding from the sea-clean concrete, the side-walks that are never finished, the dune sand drifting hotly in the front porches, the whole sense of raw impermanence, of decay that sets in before the paint is dry on the names of shops and houses, the sense that the sea is inexorably taking back, by wind and sand and sea air and the winter barrage of sand and shingle, and even by the casual trespass of sea flowers on the sidewalks, all that has been taken away from it. You read sometimes of South American towns which march as far as the edge of tropical forests and then stop, to have the finger ends of their civilisation bitten and chewed and scarred and stunted by advancing vegetation, tropical creepers, trees and flowers. This is the same effect: of sea and such sea vegetation as there is eternally fretting and scarring the concrete of civilisation, never giving it a chance to set.

So if you wanted to find sea flowers all you had to do was to walk in the hollows of the dunes that form a sea wall for the white rows of new villas or walk along the street until there was a break in the houses. On the dunes they were more natural and more beautiful than down on the vacant lots, but even there you would find magnificent clumps of orange sea poppy and blue trees of sea holly and tussocks of sea pink. In August, on the dunes which by then seemed as hot as oven bricks to your bare feet after the cool sea, sea convolvulus would be very lovely in the hollows among the sea grasses: quite large pink trumpets of morning glory growing flat on the hot sand. Sea holly, too, was lovely all over those dunes. Something like a miniature silver-blue tree, part holly, part thistle, strange and artificial, it is exactly of sea colour, blue touched with salt, and sharp as if scissored out of steel. You could gather that too on the sidewalks and the building lots, but loveliest of all, perhaps, was the orange sea poppy which grows all across shingle, dune and marsh: big handsome yellow-orange horned flowers on sea-grey leaves.

All these are true sea flowers, never really far from the shore fringe. But back in the marsh across which the little train toots God knows how many times a day, so playful and fast that you get the impression that one day it will toot beyond the black fisher huts and the new villas of Dungeness Point into the sea and go tooting across the Channel to join another little train that starts from the middle of the street at Morlaix and toots over the heather to St. Jean du Doit in Brittany, there are flowers growing in the stretches of barren shingle that are outside their proper world. For this is a strange place for foxgloves, which supposedly revel in woodland shade and coolness. Yet they grow here in great quantities in the shingle, on stretches of arid land whipped by sea wind and baked by sun. They root deeply and are startling, red-pink, on the flat yellow-brown distances of pebbles. Later in summer there is viper's bugloss here too, starved by shingle into sharp loveliness, like some hairy, handsome, overgrown forget-me-not, bright sailor blue touched with pink, brilliant on the dry summer shingle.

Here in this flat land the impression is always of the sea as the predominant force; it is always the everlasting prospective invader. Its shingle has long since been left or flung far inland, aridly beautiful, bringing with it sea flowers and a kind of sea change to such land flowers as the foxgloves. Farther along the coast, westward, where the cliffs begin again, the land dominates the sea. East of Hastings the Sussex woods, luminous with primroses and anemones in spring, come down to the edge of the cliffs. Dark thorns are beaten back like

25

torn umbrellas by the sea winds, only to burst into flower like trees of sea spray. Here you could lie on warm summer afternoons and watch the waves rolling softly in like white kittens on the shore below without feeling that what should be the precious coast of England had been cut out and parcelled up like a stick of cheap pink-and-white rock with the name of the speculator running through the middle. Farther west still, at a spot like Cuckmere Haven, the corn land too comes down to the edge of cliff and bay, the August corn sugar-brown against the blue-white plain of sky and sea beyond, and there is again the feeling that this is the coast as it should be, the natural fusion of sea and land without the barrier line of concrete speculation.

You get the same feeling—and, of course, there must be other places too—on the west coast in Scotland, where seals play in the breakers among the dark rocks, and the fuchsias bloom like trees of red and purple bells, and the smell of sun-baked seaweed is good and warm and savage all along the loch sides where the sheep come down to feed on it at low tide. The memory of such sea days excites a deep nostalgia. There is in one of Malachi Whitaker's stories a man who expresses a longing to see the sea again, and there must be many people who feel like that today, people to whom the loss of the sea, in war-time, is something almost as acute as the loss of sugar. In the last war, there being no considered danger of invasion, we kept going to the sea, and though I remember we once stayed with a lady whose ideas about food were so good that my father went out immediately after breakfast every morning and ate two boiled eggs at the restaurant round the corner, on the whole it was very good. You got then the last glimpse of another age: the age when a motor-car was a luxury, when a plane was an exciting sight, when the church parade of dresses along the promenade on Sunday mornings was still an elegant institution, when men wore straw hats and white flannels, when you lived a hundred miles from the sea and it was so like an excursion into a dream world that you began to lean out of the train window at Sevenoaks in order to persuade yourself that you could smell the sea at Eastbourne.

If you went on such excursions you know that part of your life is bound up with the landlady's aspidistra, with your father's whispered comments on the steak, with the smell of dinners floating from the big hotels along the promenade in the evenings, the concert party on the sands, the tilted sunshades of old ladies asleep in deck chairs below the gently waving bushes of pink tamarisk, the smell of cab horses waiting in the hot sun, of sea anemones in the rock pools at low tide, and the treasured piece of seaweed so carefully gathered and wrapped in a towel and taken home and hung under the verandah so that you could tell when it would rain. It is bound up with the feeling made on your bare feet by the hard tide ripples of the sand as you ran across it. It is bound up, so that any summer day on the seashore you could see grown men who had never lost the habit of it, with the joy of looking for the things the sea washes up: corks, razor shells, banners and ferns of crimson and emerald seaweed, drifts of pink and cream and blue and purple shells, frosty sea-smoothed glass, jelly fish, star fish, dead gulls. It is bound up with Madame So-and-so's singing with great heavings of her pork-white breast something from " Il Trovatore " among the palms and the plush of the Winter Gardens, with the carpet beds depicting in sombre tones of claret and grey and gold *God Save Their Majesties,* and with the day you let your grandmother's umbrella sail gloriously away on the windy sands of Skegness and nobody but you thought it funny.

Such feelings, so comically tender and trivial now, have been described as "feelings that bind our years together in a deep secretive piety." It is certain that as I go down through the Kent marshes or through the primrose villages of South Sussex there arises the strange and uneasy feeling that I am touching the fringes of another existence. I am made aware of it even by the sight of wild cabbage and the grey, handsome fronds of seakale growing in the chalk of the coast cliffs, by the sight of silver-fawn reeds left standing through autumn and winter along the marsh dykes long after the reed harvest is over. There is a touch of it, fainter, but still disturbing, as I cross the open country, much of it unenclosed, lying landward from Ramsgate, where the high summer light falling on the white fields of August barley seems sea-washed, almost candescent, on days of serene swan-white cloud, and it is increased a little as I stand in the street of some half-forgotten inland port like Faversham, and suddenly catch sight of a mast beyond a break in the dark-red houses. Time pulls back for a moment with fascinating magnetism, and as I stood once on the shores of Cape Cod, where the old-fashioned tubs of coastal passenger steamers pull in fast out of the mist and suddenly swing their tiers of light to a standstill against the wooden jetty, the same feeling took hold of me: a dead existence resurrected, momentarily claiming me back. The odd thing is that there on the Cape the houses are the same shape, the roofs as it were double-sloped, as those of the true Kent style; the old port houses are wooden and high and straggly, painted grey or cream or blue or sometimes black, as they are in the Kentish ports, and as you see them you get again the feeling of having come home. Only the crowds of big crimson and white single Indian roses straggling everywhere along the roadsides going down to the sea's edge are at all strange.

27

It is two years since I was down on the coast. You could then see the convoys of merchantmen waiting off the white point of the cliffs before entering the contraband control. A mine was tossing a little out to seaward from the wall; the fish hawkers, who had little or nothing to sell but lumps of yellow haddock, would talk to you of the dead Nazi airmen that were washed up every day on the shore. The air of decay was already hardening at a moment when it should have been lessening: ice-cream parlours closing up, amusements boarded up, painting peeling away, hotels unopened. There is no air of decay quite like the forlornness that descends on a coast town that puts up its shutters, and God and the coast army alone know what has happened to those one-street towns half-buried in sand behind the dunes, where even in peace-time sea holly and sea poppy grew in the cracks of the street. In spite of all the hard white ugliness it would be good to be there again: to see the floppy pink convolvulus open on the hot sand, the myriads of little coloured shells left after the tide, the shoals of glistening transparent jellyfish littering the shore, the bright foxgloves and viper's bugloss and sea pink flowering across the lonely marshes where people walk on the shingle in long flat-bottomed wooden shoes that are strapped on to the feet, to hear the scream of gulls and the voice of the miniature train tooting across the dykes along which kingfishers come down like blue and copper arrows to the edge of the sea, the train tooting and peeping like a grown-up toy in a toy peace-time world. Toy train, penny plaice, sea flowers, peace-time world—but it's no use getting sentimental now.

IV

Mr Pimpkins

IF your garden is just too small for a full-time gardener and just too large to be kept clean by your own hands, then you will fall victim, sooner or later, to the jobbing gardener. You first find him in the advertisement columns of the local newspaper, and it appears from the wording of the advertisement that he is practically in distress. " Two or three days a week urgently wanted. Any time. Anywhere." So you rush off to him at the first opportunity, knowing how difficult gardeners are to get, and find yourself confronted at the cottage door by his wife, who puts her nose round the door and says, " Well ?" and who when you explain says he's had practically the whole neighbourhood round that morning bothering him to go here and go there, " and he don't for the life of him know what to do, he's got too much on hand already, but, anyway, what name is it ?—he'll very like come round when he's had his tea."

You forget to point out the odd state of things by which a man who already has too much work is forced to waste money advertising for more, and you go home and wait for him to come. You wait there all evening, with the depressing feeling that he is conferring an immense favour on you by even considering your name, and in the end, of course, he does not come. He does not come, in fact, within the next ten days, and you begin to get desperate. Spring is coming on; the onions are not in; the borders are not forked; the rambler roses have not been tied. Finally you can wait no longer and you decide in desperation on an advertisement of your own. You draft this with great care and take it into the offices of the local newspaper. It will appear the following day. That evening, in the middle of supper (it is always in the middle of a meal), the maid comes in and says excuse her, please, but it's Mr Pimpkins. You cannot for the life of you remember anyone named Pimpkins, but you leave your mutton chop to get cold and go to the kitchen door, and there, looking as pleasant as if he came straight from the undertaker's, is Mr Pimpkins.

You say good-evening, not having the slightest idea who he is, and he says:

" I couldn't come afore. I ent bin well."

He does in fact look rather cadaverous and is obviously, in the language of the films, a sour puss. He is about sixty-three, with legs like scythe handles. He seems to be wearing three suits, of which he has the brown trousers of one, the blue waistcoat of another and the black jacket of the third. He wears a stiff collar without a tie and his Adam's apple lodges on it like the butt of a pump handle.

As he offers no further explanation of his presence, you say you are very sorry he ent bin well, and he says:

" Yis, it gives me such jee-up every few weeks. I've 'ad it this twelvemonth or more. Course I were in there nigh on a twelve-month."

" You were?" you say, and he says " Yis! Twelvemonth all but three weeks," as if he is rather pained that you are unfamiliar with this private and mysterious phase of his history.

You keep silence, sympathetically, and then he warms up. You ought of course to have been prepared, but you are not:

" 'Ad over three hundred injections."

" Did you indeed ?"

" Ah. Course I were in there a twelvemonth."

" Really," you say, and then, because after all it would be nice to touch at least the fringe of the subject in hand, you remark that you expect he is getting about a bit now.

" Yis, but I hadn't ought to !" he says. " I ent right, y'know. I ent right."

" It's been a tough winter for everybody," you say.

" Ah ?" he says. He put into his voice a hint of vindictiveness.
" Some 'ave bin all right. Some ent done bad. Some as I know. I
tell you."

By this time the grease has grown white and cold on your mutton
chop or the remains of it have been burnt to a cinder under the grill,
and the situation needs a piece of desperate brutality.

" Well, Mr Pimpkins," you say, " I've got an appointment in
ten minutes. How many days a week do you think you can come ?"

" Well," he says with absolutely funereal fatalism, " I han't ought
to come at all be rights."

" Oh ?"

" Be rights," he says, " I han't ought."

" Oh ?"

" I've ad so many arter me."

" Well, do you think you could come two days ? Two and a half
days ?"

" Well," he says, " I shall etta see. I shall etta see what I can
do for you. I shall etta see if I can fit y'in Thursdays an' Saturdays."

All right, you tell him, you'll leave it like that and he'll etta see.
The notion that he is conferring an immense favour on you has by this
time increased enormously and you yourself do not care any longer
whether he comes or not. But you are a civil person, and it has been
a charming spring day, and you politely mention this fact as you say
good-evening and he goes down the garden path.

" Ah !" he says, " too nice ! We shall etta suffer for it ! You see.
It ent seasonable. We shall etta suffer !"

Finally he goes and you go back to a mutton chop that has lost its
identity. You have given up caring now whether he comes or not, and
you console yourself that you have after all put in an advertisement of
your own.

Unfortunately there are no replies from your own advertisement,
and you are forced back on the hope that Mr Pimpkins will come.
And finally, all in his own good time, at leisure, at the curious hour of
twenty minutes past nine on Thursday morning, he comes.

It is a very nice morning: larks are singing over the ploughed land;
sparrows are pecking the sweet polyanthus buds. You can smell spring
in the air and it is time to sow onions.

You have a well-prepared bed under a south wall and it is there, by
early sowing, that you raise early vegetables. You point out to Mr
Pimpkins that you think it would be an excellent thing to sow a few rows
of early carrots, onions and peas in this bed, and you give him the seeds.

He ignores them utterly.

" I ent got mine in," he says.

" I'm all for early sowing," you say.

" You don't want to be in 'urry," he says.

" I'm all for early sowing," you say. " This is an early garden. We're always early."

" That rose oughta bin tied up," he says.

You agree that the rose oughta bin tied up and perhaps he will do it during the day? You also want the peas, carrots and onions sowing, and will he clear the next piece of ground of brussels sprouts, which have gone over?

" You don't wanta git them up," he says.

" They're finished," you say. " They're simply using good ground."

" I ent got mine up," he says.

This being final, you walk away. Mr Pimpkins ent got his up, so you don't get yours up. The sooner you realise that the better.

Forty minutes later you come out into the garden to see if Mr Pimpkins is finding everything to his satisfaction. Mr Pimpkins is nowhere to be seen. No seeds have been sown, no rows drawn. There are signs that the rose has been pruned, but Mr Pimpkins himself has vanished. You walk up and down the garden several times and then finally, by chance, you see Mr Pimpkins.

He is sitting in the greenhouse. It is very warm and sunny in the greenhouse and Mr Pimpkins is sitting on a box. The *Daily Mail* is spread on his knees, and on the *Daily Mail* is spread a mountainous sandwich of bread and cheese, a couple of slices of bacon and a large thermos flask of tea. Mr Pimpkins is slowly masticating his way through both the news and the food. You go into the greenhouse, struck instantly by its soft and genial warmth, to remark to Mr Pimpkins, hullo, this is where he is.

" Jist evvin me breakfast," he says.

You are wondering why Mr Pimpkins cannot have his breakfast, as other people do, in his own home and in his own time, when the problem is solved for you.

" Ent bin able to git nothing down furst thing since I were bad."

" Oh?"

" I ent arf th' eater I were," he says. " Missus used to say she wondered wheer I put it all."

As he is about to overload his stomach with a hunk of bread and cheese weighing about a quarter of a pound, which at any moment he will wash down with a pint of tea, you, too, are inclined to wonder where he puts it all.

*Mr Pimpkins is slowly masticating his way
through both the news and the food.*

33

" Ent you got no heat in your greenhouse ?" he finally says.

You apologise for the lack of heating in the greenhouse, which is only eight by fifteen, although you cannot help noticing at the same time that Mr Pimpkins looks as warm as toast. You point out that it is really only a little place for raising seeds, at which Mr Pimpkins, who appears already to have spent twenty minutes or more on his breakfast, begins an expansive reminiscence on the wonderful greenhouses of Lord Blather of Shotover, for whom he worked, man and boy, for thirty years. This reminiscence is like a river with countless tributaries. At each tributary Mr Pimpkins branches off to tell either the story of the under-butler who carried on a long and foul intrigue about the chickens kept by him for Lord Blather in 1902, or the story of Lord Blather's son, who misled a parlourmaid in 1906 and two house-maids in 1907, and against whom, for some dark reason, Mr Pimpkins still nurses an indissoluble hatred. These tributaries in turn have backwaters, and Mr Pimpkins, exploring them all, does so on the supposition that you are as familiar with Lord Blather's lineage and property, his servants and their intrigues, their families and ante-cedents, as Mr Pimpkins himself. These explorations take half an hour, by which time Mr Pimpkins condescends to return to the main theme, the whole point of which is that Lord Blather suffered with his kidneys and did not like cucumbers. Having presented you with this tremendous information he screws down his thermos flask and says: " Well, I suppose we'd better git on afore we ev dinner-time on top on us."

Dinner-time is in fact on top on us before you know anything at all. Mr Pimpkins again sits in the greenhouse to have his dinner, and at one-thirty, when you go in there to look at the petunia seedlings, you discover that the place has been fumigated by Mr Pimpkins' pipe, in which he smokes a species of shag that smells like a combination of burning horse-hooves and dung. Outside, Mr Pimpkins is calmly clipping the lonicera hedge.

You suppress your annoyance and ask why the hedge takes pre-ference over the onions, still not sown.

" Oughta bin done afore," he says.

This is final. Nothing can get past it. As the weeks go past you are to discover painfully that the garden is full of jobs that oughta bin done afore and that Mr Pimpkins will, regardless of whatever you say, do them.

After this, having been caught in the morning by the private history of Lord Blather, you retire as far from Mr Pimpkins as possible in the belief that he works better in solitude. At three o'clock you come back to the lonicera hedge, which divides the garden from the field beyond, only to discover Mr Pimpkins sharing a pipeful of shag with Charley, the horse-keeper from the farm, who is supposed to be chain-harrowing the pasture. You hear Charley say it feels like rain, and Mr Pimpkins earnestly agrees he is right. You get the impression that Mr Pimpkins would be extremely glad if it did rain, and you seize a hoe and begin to make loud and angry noises on the plot by the wall. Ten minutes later he condescends to exchange heavy farewells with Charley, as if both were going to the ends of the earth. " Well, mind ow you goo on," he says. And Charley says " Ah !" and " Gee-up !" to the horses. Mr Pimpkins then strikes practically a dozen matches, gives as many spits, and finally proceeds to clip the hedge in a cloud of evil fog.

You yourself work hard on the seed drills for the rest of the after-noon, and at four-thirty you go to the house for a hasty cup of tea. At a quarter to five you go to find Mr Pimpkins again to ask him for the seeds, only to find that he has gone home, taking the seeds in his pocket.

Mr Pimpkins continues to come all summer. Your first real shock is when you pay him at the end of the first week. The local rate used to be a shilling an hour, but it has risen to one and a penny. When you ask Mr Pimpkins how much, he says, " I got it down somewheres," and forages in his pocket for a dirty scrap of paper from which falls a shower of shag. " Semteen hours at one an' four I mek it," he says, " an' you goo arves wi' Miss Ratcliffe on insurance." You are about to protest at this monstrous statement when you remember that one of your pet hopes about the countryside is higher wages for country workers, and who are you not to set an example ? Of Miss Ratcliffe you have never heard, and you can only wonder how it is you should halve the burden of insurance with her when she employs Mr Pimpkins for four days and you for two.

Mr Pimpkins continues to confer the favour of his presence on you, weather and health permitting, every Thursday and Saturday. Some-times it rains ; sometimes " it's me back giving me gee-up again " ; some-times " Miss Ratcliffe dint gie me no peace till I went and done that cesspool job." Miss Ratcliffe emerges as a tyrant. If Mr Pimpkins dominates you, Miss Ratcliffe dominates Mr Pimpkins. Though he leaves you promptly at four forty-five, he apparently works without protest for Miss Ratcliffe until seven-thirty. He protests that March is too early for planting potatoes, but in April, when you finally plant them, it appears that Miss Ratcliffe ad ern in three weeks agoo. Your onions, which you eventually sow yourself, germinate magnificently ;

35

but you ought to see Miss Ratcliffe's. Miss Ratcliffe is always referred to as She. You suggest that Mr Pimpkins should sow French beans in boxes, but Mr Pimpkins is against it: She never does. You suggest planting out the celery, but, Good God, no, She ain't got ern out yet. Doesn't Mr Pimpkins think the tulips are good? He does; but She's got a bed of tulips Mr Pimpkins planted and you never see nothing like it. Shouldn't we grow summer cabbage? "Well," Mr Pimpkins says, "you do what you like, but She never does." In the end, oppressed either by what Miss Ratcliffe does so excellently and what she doesn't do at all, you have a violent desire to wring Miss Ratcliffe's neck.

All through the summer Miss Ratcliffe, Lord Blather, the butler who intrigued against Mr Pimpkins and, above all, the hospital, are Mr Pimpkins' dominating themes. If you ask him if he thinks it advisable to thin the peaches he goes back to the year 1903, when, it appears, the peaches at Lord Blather's were as large as pumpkins. If you complain of a cold in the head he will instantly draw your attention to the acute sufferings of stone in the kidney and layin' on me back for a twelvemonth. In short, nothing you do is so good, so bad, so successful or so painful as the things done by Miss Ratcliffe, Lord Blather, and Mr Pimpkins.

Apart from the fact that he never does as he is told, always clipping the hedge when you want seeds sown, always tying roses when you want the lawn cut, Mr Pimpkins has certain favourite horticultural pastimes. One of these is the process of settin' back. Most of your cherished shrubs, roses and perennials, it seems, want settin' back. The art of settin' back is to seize secateurs and shears and cut the most flourishing species of the garden to the ground. Anything growing with unusually healthy vigour wants settin' back. Mr Pimpkins adores this pastime, and whenever your back is turned he tries it out on the forsythia, the ceanothus, the philadelphus, the flowering currant, the buddleia, the southernwood and the rest. You come into the garden to regard with horror some treasured shrub cut to the ground. "Ah! but you wun arf see a difference," Mr Pimpkins says: than which, of course, there is no truer word. You certainly do see a difference. Unfortunately, the forsythia and the philadelphus have been cut at the wrong season and will not, now, flower for two years. The buddleia is the summer variety and not the autumn variety, and will not flower for two years either. The flowering currant is indestructible, anyway, but the ceanothus and the southernwood die in the winter. Certainly you don't arf see a difference in things!

All this time Mr Pimpkins succeeds in making you feel that he is continually conferring an immense favour on you; that you are a horti-

36

cultural ignoramus; that your garden and all it contains are quite beneath comparison with those of the best people; and that at any moment he will have to withdraw his patronage. " I ev a job to fit in everybody now," he says, " and She keeps a-bothering me to goo full time." All this appears to come rather strangely from a man who, only a month or two ago, was begging by advertisement for extra work, but you let it pass.

From this time onward Mr Pimpkins' hours become increasingly erratic. He arrives at ten past nine and leaves at five to twelve; he arrives at one twenty and knocks off at five. He comes for only a day and a half, then a day, and finally half a day a week. By the time he has lit his pipe thirty times, 'ad me mite o' breakfast, and set back the *Rosa Moyseii*, which in consequence is reduced to nothing, it is time to goo 'ome an' ev me bit o' dinner.

Finally there arrives a week when Mr Pimpkins does not come at all. You can hardly believe this, and you wait another week for confirmation. He still does not come, and the next day you hear, by means of the village Gestapo, that Mr Pimpkins is working for Miss Ratcliffe full time.

On the day you hear that announcement you go out into the garden. You walk up and down. The air is free of shag, and in the greenhouse Mr Pimpkins, who ent arf th' eater he were, is no longer trying to get down enough food for a cart horse. There is no Lord Blather, no butler, no Miss Ratcliffe. But this is not all. There is another difference. It is more subtle; it seems to be part of yourself and you cannot define it.

For a long time you cannot understand what it is or why it affects you as it does. Then suddenly you do understand. You realise that the garden is your own: it belongs not to Mr Pimpkins any longer, but to you; you can do what you like with it and not as Mr Pimpkins says you must do.

And for the first time for several months you are happy.

V

The Future Garden

MR PIMPKINS, the survival of one generation, casts his shadow forward over the new generations of the countryside. Like the great house, Mr Pimpkins is a dying survival. I have set him down as something of a comic figure, but he is really a serious figure. He dominates and victimises those of limited income who, for rest or pleasure or escape from the bomb and the town, come to live in the country. In the past, in the days of the great house, servants had little independence. Their life was service. But Mr Pimpkins has independence; he works when he will and for whom he likes; he has no ideals of service and sets out deliberately to create the impression that he is conferring a favour on those who employ him. Mr Pimpkins, like many servants, is really ignorant, prejudiced, selfish and stubborn: which is not to say that many employers are not ignorant, prejudiced, selfish and stubborn too. We are not divided into classes by incomes and politics, but by shades of character. There are certainly good Mr Pimpkinses as well as bad Mr Pimpkinses. The point is, can we do without them? We are talking much of the future of the countryside. Are we to encourage the Mr Pimpkinses in that future? Are we to continue to employ ignorant people—there are Mrs Pimpkinses, unhappily, too—to do the most important tasks of the garden and the household?

For myself I hope that, in my own future in the countryside, there will be no Mr Pimpkins. I do not need Mr Pimpkins to tell me how to tie up the American Pillar, how to sow carrots, that petunia seed does not need to be covered with soil. I have taken the trouble to find out these things myself. And as with all knowledge acquired by your own experience, the results are happier. A little groundsel among the zinnias, perhaps, a flush of dandelions on the lawn—but does it matter? A garden is the expression of its owner's character. But Mr Pimpkins, if you let him, will impose himself on the place. Are the borders untidy? Better that they should be untidy and glorious, with your ideas of colour, than tidy and carefully regimented, with Mr Pimpkins'. And Mr Pimpkins, you will find, is rarely imaginative. His gardening schemes, few enough anyway, repeat themselves. Whereas you, if you are a person at all, will expand, develop, change. You are never satisfied.

As I look at the garden in which I now sit writing I see a great deal of myself. The garden, eleven years ago only a meadow of weeds, is now tall and lush with trees and flowers. In eleven years I have changed; so has the garden, because the garden is myself. I see the record of enthusiasms gone stale, of bad mistakes, of carelessness, of a desire for quick effect. I would like to make a new garden. The old is very dear to me, but in the new one, I fondly imagine, there would be no mistakes. A lot of things I once thought were good, desirable and, alas! artistic, would not be there; a lot of things I once thought were ordinary, outmoded and common would find a place.

First, the situation. I have never regretted a house that had its back to the road and its face to its garden. Why have the kitchen over-looking the borders, and the best windows of the house overlooking the bus route? My house would face south, of course, but a south un-hampered by trees. I should want a long, tranquil, unbroken reach of countryside, both to south and west, running down to the sea. I like more than anything else about the English sky that white, candescent sea light that is reflected upward against high cloud on hot summer afternoons, and I should want also to see the sunset. So I would be on a small hill, above trees, and not in a comfortable hollow, below them.

There would be several things in this garden that were not in the old; and several things not there that were in the old. With two of the great fashions of the time, for instance, I would have nothing to do.

39

There would be no rock garden, and there would be no crazy paving. In one district in Kent a rough local marble is quarried. This Bethersden marble, the huge time-smoothed blocks of which form the pavements in that lovely Kentish village, wears to a fine brown-white surface and is, except for London paving stone, the best crazy paving material I know. We accordingly made paths of it—with, as I see it, tiresome and expensive results. The upkeep of the paths in summer is expensive, and everybody hates the job of weeding them. We have tried several other paving materials: gravel, concrete, ashes, grass. All are bad, since all need attention. It was not until eight or nine years after the garden was made that we forgot about artistic pride and made our first really satisfactory, permanent and labour-saving path. It was straight; designed for use; it had no artiness about it. It was made of old bricks, and the bricks were cemented in. The amount of labour since expended on it could be reckoned in minutes: a sweeping once a week and no more. Even Mr Pimpkins, who derided most of our efforts by silence or damned them with faint praise, thought well of it.

But Mr Pimpkins did not think well of the rock garden, and for once we confess that Mr Pimpkins' reasons were right. "Rock gardens," said Mr Pimpkins, "mek a lotta work." We might add that they make a lot of work for a short season of flowering. Ten years ago we spent much time reading the works of Farrer, Jekyll, Robinson and others, and we thought the revolution in English gardening an excellent thing. Now we are not so sure. We were so sure, at that time, that a rock garden was the right and proper thing that we expended much labour, time and money in making a good one. The stone was right, the situation was right, the construction was right. No almonds in a cake for us. What we did not stop to consider was whether the soil was right, or whether we could seriously expect rare and beautiful alpines, whose natural habitat was 10,000 feet of ice and snow and blazing sun, to flourish and survive at 300 feet in a climate where it sometimes seemed that rain fell on 300 days of the year.

Our trouble was largely soil. Our garden lies on that narrow Kentish escarpment under the North Downs that contains some of the finest cherry orchards in England, and is said to contain some of the finest soil in the world. This was never a soil for alpines. It was moist and rich. It grew Siberian wallflowers in plants a yard across; our first Canterbury bells looked less like flowers than the wind-filled bloomers of middle-aged ladies hanging out on wash-day. The soil that could produce such giants was wrong for alpine midgets. They grew lush and died. And the survivals, we discovered, were not alpines at all. They were small and charming, but they could be grown just as well on the stone edges of borders as on the stone hillocks we had so expensively made. And the things which survived winter after winter were, we noted, the things which had survived in England for a long time. In short, what we were really doing, after a few years, was growing a number of small herbaceous plants among rocks and persuading ourselves that the result was a section of the Dolomites.

Today, as I look at it, the only real failure in the garden is the rock garden. Designed as part of the revolt against snobbery, it became, we confess, a piece of snobbery itself. It was an expression of the " imitation of nature " school. It was held to be vastly more natural than bedding out.

Now a garden, as I see it, is an artificially created thing: a place where one grows flowers, fruit, trees and vegetables that are the result of hybridisation, selection and civilisation. It is not a reproduction of nature, any more than a house is a reproduction of nature, because there is nothing in nature like it. It is in fact a conflict against nature. In nature there are no pergolas, no terraces, no walls, no borders, no beds. These, like so much that we take for granted in the English countryside, are men-made ideas. The " imitation of nature " school, which very significantly made its appearance about the same time as the William Morris school of this and that, made a great demand for naturalness in gardens and was highly scornful of formality. The one was good taste; the other bad. I now confess that it seems to me just as bad taste to erect a section of the Alps outside the drawing-room window because it imitates nature, as it is to have a rectangular bed of petunia and antirrhinum because it doesn't. Indeed, the Alps idea seems to me rather more pretentious, and to be more condemned, than the other.

A suspicion that the growing of exclusive alpines might be a snobbish affair first came to me on an evening when one of those alpine enthusiasts was showing me his garden. It was a very good garden, and contained many beautiful things. Did he grow delphiniums ? I asked. " Heavens," he said, " *anybody* can grow delphiniums. *I* want to grow what other people can't."

I went away from this garden with my faith in alpines and alpine enthusiasts much shaken. Here was a man who wanted to grow *Gentiana Farreri* not simply because it was beautiful, but because it was eclectic and because his neighbours didn't, and who would have been immensely scornful of the local butcher growing a twelve-inch dahlia and trying to beat all comers at the local show. Here, I thought, is a man who cares less about flowers than about being different.

So gradually, because my soil was not right, because I didn't want to imitate nature, and largely because I had to expend a great deal of work for a very short season of flowering, my fondness for rock gardens cooled. There are many alpines and sub-alpines I love; there are many alpines, which have flowered once with me and died, that I would give anything to grow again. But most of the best survivals on my rock garden—the crocus species, the phloxes, the saxifrages, the alpine asters, the lithospermums—can be successfully grown elsewhere. They can in fact be better grown on a steep dry wall.

If the situation of the new garden is right, therefore, there will be no rock garden. Instead there will be a dry stone wall, facing south, with a dry brick path running beneath it, so that I can walk and work there in winter and early spring. The wall will grow many common alpines, and some rarities, perhaps, to perfection, and on the crest of it will run the little early crocuses, *Iris reticulata,* and the big exotic cream and scarlet tulips from Turkestan. In summer, against all the canons of what is called good taste, I shall probably sow dwarf rose godetia or, better still, giant petunias that will fall down the wall in cascades of lilac and purple and white and mauve.

Just as there will be no rock garden and no crazy paving, so there will, I think, be no pergola. The primary purpose of a pergola being shade, and the English climate being an infuriating combination of east wind, west wind and funereal cloud, there seems little point in erecting an expensive structure for roses when those roses can be grown rather better in another way. The primary trouble with pergolas is that they fall down; the secondary trouble is that one needs a balloon in order to see the best of the flowers. Both are discouraging. My first pergola was built of beech poles, and the man who put it up said, "Mark my words, it'll fall down," and it did. My second pergola was built of sturdier stuff, chestnut and ash, and I myself said it would fall down, and it did. My third pergola was built of brick and oak, and the man who put it up said it would last for ever. I agreed with him, and it fell down the next winter.

James Thurber, the American humorist, has a story called *The Night the Bed Fell on Father.* We, in our family, have a memory that might be called *The Day the Pergola Fell on Mother.* Our brick pergola was an ambitious affair: long considered, a luxury, a proud addition to the garden. The material for its twenty-four pillars and its oak cross-pieces came from one of those great houses that our generation is sweeping away. The material was excellent and cheap. We made the fatal mistake—the fatal mistake in gardening and building—of trying to erect it cheaply. The erection, we regret to say, was done by one of our several Mr Pimpkinses. We discovered too late that it took just as long as if it had been done by an expert, was just as expensive, and about ten times less satisfactory. It looked well, the roses grew on it with great luxuriance, but finally, on a windy winter day with a sixty-mile-an-hour gale blowing from the south-west, my wife turned suddenly from hanging out the clothes to see twenty of the twenty-four pillars falling in a catastrophic broadside across the herbaceous borders. There was a noise like the bursting of an immense sea wave against a breaker, and the work of weeks, the roses of years, lay in a chaotic mess.

And in the end, of course, we had very shamefacedly to ask the experts to put it up again. We might just as well have asked them in the first place; indeed much better. We spent most of the time apologising for the previous workmanship; we spent exactly twice as much as we need originally have done; and the only comforting thing about it all was that we lost only a single rose. But we learnt a bitter, bitter lesson.

And that lesson was that it is better to have the best and pay for it than have the worst and pay double. So in the new garden there will be no pergola. The climbing roses will be grown against a stout oak fence; they will be trained flat, so that when they bloom we do not need a balloon to see them. And the fence will be erected by experts.

Indeed we shall go to what seems like the luxurious expense of having everything done by experts. Mr Pimpkins will not be there, spending half the morning evvin me breakfast, nor trying to impose his own ideas on ours. Mr Pimpkins seems cheap; the expert seems expensive. But time only shows us that for what we have paid successive pipe-smoking, breakfast-munching, deprecating Mr Pimpkinses we could have had the garden planned and planted by experts.

So next time we shall go to an expert. We shall say that we have our gardening ideas, just as we have our architectural ideas, and that we will pay him to carry them out. He will be our gardening architect. We shall tell him the things we want, and how we want them, and we shall watch that he does them. The imagination will be ours; the construction his. The bill, when it comes in, will seem large, extravagant and impossible, but in the six months that the work has taken we shall not have been hunting in the greenhouse for Mr Pimpkins, or wondering if Mr Pimpkins is coming to work, or if he's bin laid up this last fortnit wimme kidneys. We shall, we hope, have been doing our own work, and perhaps, if things go well, earning enough money to pay the expert.

No rock garden, then, no crazy paving, no pergola, no Mr Pimpkins. And in their place, we confess, some heresies. The first of these is bedding out. Now bedding out, so derided by Robinson and Jekyll, was one of the big red sins of the Victorians. Like most fashions, it seemed unbelievably bad to the succeeding generation. It was identified with geranium Paul Crampel, blue lobelia, yellow calceolaria and white marguerite: the suburban and small town fashion than which, I confess, there was never a more hideous colour combination anywhere; or with *God Save Their Majesties* in grey, blue, magenta and orange carpet plants on the front at the seaside: a fashion which died, happily, with the bandeau, the boater and the church parade. Because these were bad, the reformers said, the whole idea was bad. So it was away with scarlet geraniums and carpet beds, and away, unfortunately, with fuchsias and picotee carnations and auriculas and pom-pom chrysanthemums and ivy geraniums, and indeed many of the flowers that were our grandparents' pride. With the bad went the good, and before our generation had arrived many of the good things had practically vanished from all but remote country gardens.

Rectangular and gaudy: these were apparently the watchwords for bedding out. Victorian materialism—you might think sometimes that the age had only one characteristic—liked brass notes and scarlet splashes. But Victorian love of the miniature endeared itself to the picotee and the fuchsia and the auricula. Today you will find them cultivated by specialists.

Bedding out, indeed, is not a bad thing. It was simply that the flowers that went into the beds were the wrong flowers. The English climate is a curious affair—today, in August, is as dark and glowering as January, the sky full of rain and turmoil—but it enables us to grow a greater range of flowers than any country in the world. An enormous number of these flowers are not hardy: they flower and die in a summer. It was for these, as I see it, that the bedding-out idea was devised. You could grow polyanthus, wallflowers, tulips, daffodils, auriculas, squills and hyacinths in spring and follow them by petunias, zinnias, godetias, clarkias, snapdragons, asters and phloxes in summer. If you liked you could even follow these with chrysanthemums. You had flowers from March to November.

What was wrong with that? Oh! the reformists said, it is, for one thing, too easy. And for another it isn't gardening at all: it's geometry. But the easier gardening is the better I, for one, like it. And it so happens that the well-planned, well-established herbaceous border is no place for annuals. Filling up the gaps is an unsatisfactory way of growing some of the choicest things we have. Annuals need sun, light and space: like children they are happier together.

Years of trying to combine herbaceous borders and beds of annuals, with generally poor results, have made me see this. In the new garden the two will be sternly separated. Beds will continue the formality of the house; herbaceous borders will light up the distances. Nor would the beds contain only annuals. There are some perennials which are happier in specially prepared beds by themselves. I think often of a bed of Chinese pæonies, the young leaves almost the colour of copper beeches in spring, and cream narcissus growing among them and dying down before the pæonies flower in June; and then after the pæonies have flowered, groups of *Lilium regale, L. speciosum* and *L. tigrinum* rising in succession from the dark foliage. Properly planted, with good materials, such a bed would last and give pleasure for years. If you preferred early daffodils to narcissus, or *Iris reticulata* to daffodils, you would have flowers from February to October.

On these lines you could work out many ideas: sometimes annuals alone, sometimes perennials alone, sometimes the two together. Beds have also the virtue of being easy to work. The soil, if you are growing annuals, gets decently turned twice a year, and it is pleasant and clean to work on it in winter. Far easier than the rock garden, where weeds lock themselves in the fissures of the rocks, and your choicest fairy campanula gets suffocated by a thistle. Moreover, if you like semi-alpines or dwarf plants which pass for alpines in England, there seems to be nothing to prevent your growing them in beds too. The finest bed of *Gentiana acculis* I ever saw was growing in a good honest strip, on the flat, like parsley.

As for alpines, we recall now that perhaps the greatest shock to our horticultural pride was given us by a Swiss maid we once had. The rock garden was then really the proud spot of the garden, and had not become the disgraceful affair of seedlings and weeds that war and waning enthusiasm have made it today. We used to lead visitors to it with a kind of casual deliberation. In that way we led the Swiss maid. To our horror she burst out laughing. When we asked her what was the matter she merely pointed to many of the best of our spring treasures and shrieked: "Mais elles sont les mauvaises herbes!" To her it seemed immensely comic that we had raised up a pitiful imitation of her native Alps, only to plant in it the weeds that were the bane of every vineyard back home. And she never afterwards failed to be awfully amused by our collection of *mauvaises herbes*.

Whenever we hear gardeners talking of alpines we remember the Swiss maid. The term rock plant is something like the term poetry: it covers a lot of altitude. Most rock plants are, alas! to some peasant in the Pyrenees or the French Alps, or even in Chile, nothing but *les mauvaises herbes* of the lower valleys. They are mown down as callously as the meadows of autumn crocus are mown in the Tyrol in September.

45

This does not lessen their beauty or value as flowers; it ought merely to make for a greater accuracy of description. About one in a hundred varieties of plant grown on average English rock gardens is, I suppose, a true alpine. Even that one is short-lived. The true alpine, of the really high Alps, is very difficult to grow in cultivation. Pure icy miniatures do not really belong to the English pastoral, and it is worth noting that of tens of thousands of Himalayan species brought home by the plant collector Kingdon Ward, only a tiny fraction succeeded well enough in England to be a commercial proposition. And of these the two most famous, *Lilium regale* and *Meconopsis Baileyi*, were much more herbaceous than alpine.

Our national inclination, dictated largely, of course, by climate and soil, is for the intermediate. In a country too damp for alpines, too temperate for tropical things, we love plants of cool strong growth and colour. Look at all times of the year at the average English garden: the colours are cool and intermediate. It is not entirely taste which revolts from geranium Paul Crampel or the massive scarlet sculpture of August dahlias. The colour is pitched too high for the tender English light. We feel always a need for toning down.

So, because one geranium is impossibly scarlet and because one section of dahlias is impossibly flamboyant, we incline to reject them all. But in my new garden, if ever it is made, there will be a place for geraniums of kinds, and there will be dahlias. I shall hope for a terrace facing south, built of good cream stone, and down the walls I shall have geranium Charles Turner, or one of the kind, fall in tender pink ropes all summer, and on top of the wall there will be tumbling rows of fuchsia, purple and crimson, pink and white, white and salmon, dancing like sprays of Chinese lanterns. The reds and purples will be beautiful against the stone, and children will come to pop open the fuchsia buds, or my own children pop them open now, and see the purple heart burst open in the sun. Or instead of fuchsias I shall have the big trumpet petunias that are like satin Victorian ball dresses, with plum bloom on the black purples, the magentas, the pinks and the whites of their floppy petals. Why do flowers go out of fashion? There has never been an annual yet to do more than the petunia can, or do it more beautifully. You raise it in March and plant it out in May. You put out a hundred plants and the first day there are three blooms. The next day there are six, the next day fifteen; in a week you have sixty. All summer they go on happily increasing, until you have something that is really a bed: a thick eiderdown of flowers that lasts until November.

Even Mr Pimpkins, we recall, secretly admired our petunias, of which the old Rose of Heaven was always good. We found it seeding itself, year after year, in the cracks of the crazy paving. We remember, too, that we gave some to an old lady who potted them with great patience and kept them blooming in a window all winter. We were never very good at things in pots. Pots are for the very old: the water jug, the carpet slippers, the gentle daily round among the fuchsias and the ferns, a world in which the discovery of thrip on the drawing-room cineraria is the day's most shattering event. The only things in pots at which we have excelled are chrysanthemums, and in the new garden there will certainly be more and more chrysanthemums.

It is odd that almost the most magnificent of the year's flowers should be almost the last to bloom. There was a time when we lost interest in the flower garden, heaven knows why, in September. Now we have arranged it so that one of the best of all displays is in October: Michaelmas daisies, heleniums, late golden rod, dahlias, and the second blooming of many things. To this we always wanted to add chrysanthemums, and accordingly planted outdoor varieties in the borders. By September they were lost in the seas of helenium and rudbeckia and mullein and phlox and a score of other robust and gorgeous things, and when they finally bloomed they were lying on the earth. It was this that made us take up late chrysanthemums in pots, with results so good that even Mr Pimpkins, who used to goo in fer chrysanths a lot afore I 'ad me operation, thought they were splendid.

We first began with a couple of dozen mixed varieties with which we made our first and almost fatal mistake. We knew that chrysanthemums were rich feeders: so we would give them caviare. From the local poultry keeper we therefore got a load of used bacterised peat that had been well impregnated with fowl droppings. Into this neat and almost lethal mixture we potted the young chrysanthemums. They seemed to thrive well for a week, and then their leaves began to turn brown and drop off. Soon they were naked. It was now almost the end of June and the situation desperate. Finally I pulled out one of the plants. The stench was impossible; the soil was a foul and sickly mess; the plant was almost rootless. I repotted every plant and learned my first lesson.

That summer and the next, by visiting nurserymen who grew chrysanthemums, I learned other lessons. I learned never to fill up my pots with soil, but to leave an inch and a half for August top dressings. I learned to stake well and early, because staking helps growth and because crooked stems are useless. I learned not to coddle, nor to apply fussy remedies. I grew things well and naturally, and I even broke all the rules by growing the plants for two years in the same pots, with results, the second year, that were better than the first. I knew nothing about disbudding, timing and stopping; first crowns or second crowns. The first year I grew all first crown buds, with sometimes only one flower to a plant. They looked good enough for the church altar. The second year I grew some first crowns and some seconds, and the seconds had a kind of natural homeliness that was very happy. I never knew if I was doing right, and used to spend hours over expert works trying to learn the art of timing and stopping, which varies with each variety. Unfortunately for these intentions my two small boys had carried off all the labels in order to make an air-raid shelter in the middle of the onion bed, a game since superseded by the making of tank traps among the hybrid perpetuals, and I no longer knew which variety was which. The result was that I had to use my own gumption, which is practically the first and last rule about all gardening anyway, and finally, when I went back to the local nurseryman to compare my amateur results with his it was to discover that he never troubled about timing or second crowns at all, but apparently took a bud here and there as the fancy moved him. His flowers looked less specialised than mine, and were really, on his own admission, less good than they should have been; but I have no doubt they had lacked the many hours of gentle contemplation I had given mine on dull September evenings in the little greenhouse where they were packed so tight that I had to shut myself in for an hour before I could water them.

And with them we spanned the dark gap of the flowering year. The latest of them still bloomed in January. They linked up with *Viburnum fragrans,* crowded all winter with tender shell-pink rosettes by the porch outside, with winter honeysuckle and Christmas roses, with the first starry lemon aconites. They helped to take us over into spring.

So in the new garden there will be many of them. And we have learned some new tricks. One is that the rather finicky business of taking early cuttings under glass is not really necessary. This year, most of our time being spent among Stirling bombers and the men who fly them, we took no cuttings, but simply tore off rooted shoots from the old stools and set them out in the vegetable garden like cabbages. The result in health and vigour made a lie of every chrysanthemum book I ever read.

And so tastes change, or appear to change. You pass through a phase in which the minute charms of campanulas seem to satisfy everything, and you emerge captivated by the white bosoms of chrysanthemum Blanche de Poitou. This, you say, is the measure of my development. I can't help wondering if it is so. If I think for a

With the chrysanthemums we spanned
the dark gap of the flowering year.

49

moment about most of my deepest affections among flowers I discover that all, or practically all, go back to childhood. They seem to emerge, in my thirties, as changes over the tastes of my twenties. In reality, I feel, they are confirmations of the affections of thirty years ago.

Yes; they are all there: the white Madonna lilies of my father's first garden; the pink primroses, the ostrich asters, the tea roses of my grandfather's; the chrysanthemums of the dark little seed shop where the roof was so low that the raffia brushed your hair as it hung from the rafters; the hyacinths of my great-grandmother's drawing-room in winter; the perpetual roses, the pure yellow violas; the fuchsias, the pelargoniums and the petunias of country windows; the tobacco plants heavy with scent on darkening summer evenings.

Scent is the extraordinary power that flicks you back, in a split second, through a quarter of a century of confused recollection, to a pin point in a childhood that is clearer than the moment in which you stand remembering. If I bruise the leaf of a geranium I am back instantaneously in a Bedfordshire village in a year when the internal-combustion engine was about to start in the English countryside a greater revolution than the repeal of Corn Laws or the imposition of enclosures. The window of the little house looks out on a wood and in the foreground is the garden. There are Maiden's Blush roses by the door, and gooseberries as large as golf balls on the bushes beyond the mauve flowers of the potatoes. In the window are the red geraniums and in the chair under the window is my Uncle Silas, as likely as not half-canned, telling the story of the cook who did not agree with the way he had of showing his affection under Lord St. John's damsons.

It has been said that what we need from science is more knowledge about man; and it certainly seems an astounding thing that we appear to have no explanation of the way the scent of flowers, itself an abstract and ephemeral thing, can photograph itself on the mind of man in so forcible and permanent a way that a breath of corresponding scent, twenty or thirty or even fifty years afterwards, can make instantaneous contact with the first association more perfectly than amplified sound waves are picked up by a receiver. The connection between sight and memory seems simpler; something visual and material is photographed, imprinted on the mind. How can something invisible, untouchable and intangible, like the fragrance of pinks or the odour of chrysanthemums, persist through years with visual and particular associations?

Do scientists ponder over these things in obscure laboratories? I hope they do. The associations of memory are largely sentimental, but if we are to know more about man we might well begin with a scientific investigation of sentimental things. Is there any other device than the animal brain that will record fragrances through visual pictures that can be re-transmitted after years? The whole subject seems suddenly so simple that it terrifies me: yet it might well belong to the realm of those simple inquisitive events like the fall of the apple in Newton's garden or the harvest mice in Gilbert White's study in Selborne.

So there would be plenty of scent in the new garden. We should reserve, among roses, a high place for hybrid perpetuals. This is not because new roses are not scented—an absurd fallacy in which the public loves to persist—but because we like the shapelessness, the blowsiness and the deep generosity of the perpetuals, which are also less temperamental with us than the modern hybrid teas. Also they grow into trees, not dwarf three-stemmed bushes of which the flowers, however glorious, are less than eighteen inches from the earth. We like the blonde operatic grandeur of Frau Karl Drushki, the rather military stature of Captain Hayward. We should have more of their companions, in beds separate from the slender girl friends of today. We notice that they grow not only stronger, but cleaner; show less tendency to black spot and dying in winter. Their scent is ripe and depthless; it comes up from a well. Why did the perpetuals die out of favour? We fancy the craze for flower shows and exhibitions had much to do with it. The perpetual rose never has that delicate pointed breast of a bud seen in the best modern rose; it has a generous and uncorseted look. It went out with the ostrich feather and the boa and the fashion for wearing buttonholes.

To the outmoded fashions of the Victorians we should, therefore, give quite a lot of consideration in the new garden. They were good gardeners; their choice was more limited than ours. They grew many things better; their plants seem to have been less troubled by disease. We could learn much from them.

But we have learnt most from ourselves, from our own mistakes, our own ambition, our own lack of care, and above all from our own independent craving to do a thing because we wanted to. Mr Pimpkins frustrated in us a natural desire for experiment. It was our rule, until Mr Pimpkins appeared, to taste new potatoes in May. But no charge of dynamite could induce Mr Pimpkins to plant before the second week in April. "You doant wanta git taters too early," said Mr Pimpkins.

But this was just the point. We did want to get them too early: the earlier the better. We always did get them early. "Yis, but you'll cop out," Mr Pimpkins warned us, "with a frorst." "Never mind," we said. "Ah! all right," said Mr Pimpkins, "all right." So finally we let ourselves be frightened and we failed to put in our early potatoes when we should. That spring, as it proved, was the most frostless spring we ever remembered.

And from this emerges our real plan for the future garden. We shall plant it how we like and where we like, and we shall plant in it what we like, and be damned, very politely of course, to Mr Pimpkins and everyone else. And that, from our point of view, would seem to be a very good thing.

VI

The Garden on Leave

ALL summer, between weeks with Spitfires and Beaufighters and odd visits to Poles and Czechs on lonely aerodromes and the bombed cities of the west, I have managed to snatch an hour or two in the old garden. Today I see that Miss Rose Macaulay has been writing on the Consolations of War, an essay a year or two old, no doubt, with its background of blitz and shelters and crowded tubes, and the naked bath hanging by a thread of pipe from the bomb-split bathroom. But certainly war has its consolations, as it has also its confirmations. And it has special consolations for those who are driven away from the country to aerodromes and lonely units and gun sites and the blitzed towns. It sends them back with a clearer, sharper eye.

Also it shifts the direction of the eye. Ten years ago we were always at the rock garden, watching the progress of a new miniature; we went to bed with alpine catalogues and read with the light on and the window open and the dusty summer moths bouncing in against the glowing bulb. This summer we have never looked at the rock garden; we have spent most of our precious hours of leave contemplating cauliflowers, admiring

53

pea blossom and feeding with rich vintages of sheep dung the pears and peaches. We have been to bed with fruit catalogues, old Victorian manuals on pomology, and have read with the window closed and no moths bouncing in, and the only sound the wail of the siren coming up the valley.

The result is we have found our consolations. Quite the most smiling and flattering letter of the war comes from a girl to whom we sent a box of onions; quite the most envious looks have come from those people to whom we mentioned, with casual point, that we were about to gather our peaches. The leek, once a terribly despised vegetable, made new friends for us with a rapidity only equalled, twenty-five years ago, by the Worcester Pearmains with which we sought to appease large and very aggressive boys at a new school. " Would you like a lettuce ?" has had on visitors something of the stimulant effect we once observed only after " Would you like a cocktail ?" A number of horse vegetables, notably the swede, the kohlrabi and the kale, have all become quite aristocratic.

But the great consolations are that we have been successful, at last, with fruit. So successful that much of our time is now spent going round the garden walls and wondering if we dare secretly root out the ceanothus, the Mermaid roses, the forsythias, the abutilons, the clerodendrons, the wistarias, the bignonia and other tender things in order to replace them with peaches and pears and possibly a nectarine and an apricot or two. We grew up with the fixed illusion that all these fruits, with the possible exception of the pear, were luxury fruits only to be grown in the gardens of aristocrats. It needed a war to dispel the illusion and show us that we could grow them ourselves.

To us the pear is the queen of fruits. So our first trees, ten years ago, were Conference and Doyenne du Comice. It is said that one needs a special dispensation from the Almighty to grow pears well, and reluctantly after some years we concluded, not perhaps surprisingly, that the Almighty had no special dispensations for us. Conference and Doyenne du Comice bloomed well, but as far as our palates were concerned might have remained virgin. Once we had a crop of Conference, but the Battle of Britain started as they ripened, and the birds had a feast during our temporary evacuation. Now and then a crabbed and miserable Doyenne du Comice managed to survive until September, too crusty and juiceless even for the wasps to eat, and then fell miserably off the tree.

Then we decided to introduce a Duchess. We are not very well acquainted with the fertility of Duchesses generally, but Pitmaston Duchess comes of very lusty Victorian ancestry and produces fruit as

54

Once we had a crop of Conference.

55

large as a bomb. We felt, anyway, that our barren Doyenne and empty Conference needed the stimulant of another line. The Duchess was beautiful. Her leaves are heavy and dark and glossy and her blossom is extraordinarily pure white and large. To our delight she conceived the first year. Unfortunately the Almighty even then withdrew the dispensation so reluctantly given. One cannot be blessed with everything, and it seemed, at last, a choice between pears and children. For on a day in July, three months too early, we saw our two sons emerging from the fruit garden, carrying in their hands the pears so long part of our dreams. We never quite understood why they looked so pleased with themselves.

After that we gave up hoping for a dispensation. We decided to put our faith, as we have done on other occasions with disturbing success, in material things. We would see what protection, pruning shears, and a diet of liquid manure would do. The Doyenne had after all been planted ten years: it was probably on the wrong stock, it had never yielded an eatable fruit, and our only consolation came from East Malling, where at the Research Station I asked, " I wish you would tell me what's wrong with my Doyenne du Comice," to which they simply replied: " We wish you would tell us what is wrong with ours."

From this I gathered that Doyenne du Comice, like blackcurrants, Royal Sovereign strawberries, Lloyd George raspberries, was either in a decline, about to revert, or just the subject of another miserable modern disease. These unhappy things always happen to aristocrats, and Doyenne du Comice has been called the *lafite* of all pears. The Duchess meanwhile looked rich and prodigal with health, and in the spring of this year was covered with what I think must be the largest and handsomest of all pear bloom. Doyenne du Comice is, of course, self-sterile, but no pear with a beautiful name like Pitmaston Duchess could be anything but self-fertile. Conference is also fertile. The weather was good and dry and frostless, and the bees worked well: so well that finally, in a brief spell of leave, we were able to come home and find one of the war's nicest consolations. The dispensation had been given. The three trees had a final setting of about a couple of hundred pears.

But that, we thought, is not enough. Pears grow exceptionally well in France. The French would naturally have the correct attitude towards a sensuous and succulent fruit like the pear, and it is no accident, I think, that there is a wine called Château de Clou Vougeot, a very beautiful black-red rose named after it, and a pear called Marie Louise whose perfume is exactly that of the rose. Wine, dark red roses, aromatic pears: they belong to a sensuous people. In England the word sensuous has come to mean something slightly forbidden and not in the best taste, and the pear is therefore, perhaps, not so much favoured here as the cooler, sharper, more astringent apple, whose fullest sweetness comes only with patience and time. The pear is very much of summer and sunlight, a warm and juicy and full-living fruit, running lusciously with aroma and sweetness. It is essentially a southern thing, with some of the ripe gold and mellowness and sensuality of French painting.

But pears need not only sunlight but water. Perhaps more than anything, after all, they need affection. So the Doyenne and the Duchess, both on a south wall, were treated to three or four waterings a week, and in most weeks a bucket of liquid manure, the colour of pale coffee; and they were treated, whenever I got home on leave, to a few moments of contemplation, in the early mornings when the dew was on the leaves and the bloom was slightly blue on the caromel ripeness of the fruit, or in the evenings after watering. Neither process is recommended in the books. Indeed summer manuring is, we believe, quite wrong. But the best gardening practice, however unorthodox, is that which gives results. And we observe now that with manure and mothering the Doyenne bears really magnificent, firm and sun-touched pears, and that the Duchess flourishes in pregnant splendour. So it seems after all that perhaps one doesn't need a special dispensation for pears, but only the sense to see that they get sunlight, tenderness and water.

We, at any rate, are going to plant more pears. We shall marry them carefully, the sterile with the fertile, the early with the late. We are seduced by the French femininity of their names—Josephine de Malines, Marguerite Marrilat, Marie Louise, Louise Bonne de Jersey, Belle Julie, Duchesse de Bordeaux—and their sensuous succulence —Glou Morceau, Beurre Superfin, Durondeau, Jargonelle, Winter Orange. It will be one of the consolations of war to come home after weeks with bombers and fighters to see the white pear blossom and smell its slightly southern and exotic odour of vanilla and see the bees on the red stamens, and then from August to October to watch the colour, warm chestnut-red on the Marie Louise, golden-green on the Pitmaston Duchess, maturing on the fruit. And it will be one of the consolations of middle age and still more of old age, we hope, to sit a long time at the dining-table on October evenings, with the yellow candlelight falling on the pears and the mahogany and the silver, and to take a knife to a pear and peel it with reverence and suck at it and let the juice run down chin and hands. We hope to sit for a long time, peeling and munching, munching and sucking, relishing our pears with reflective affection, breathing in the aroma of summer through the cool, sweet, glistening flesh. The curls of golden peel will lie on the plate and we shall turn the black pips over with the knife edge. By that time our teeth will probably not be very good; we shall leave the apples to the younger generation. Pears, even if one does not need a special dispensation to grow them, are to the old a dispensation in themselves. The young can bite into an apple as hard as a mangel-wurzel and as negative as a cucumber. The pear was made for those whose teeth are gone, whose hands are slow and who, having once sat down, do not want to get up in a hurry.

And it is right, perhaps, that our love of pears should also go back to childhood. We remember the colossal pear tree by the monastery, on a house dated 1745, in the town where we grew up, the pears as big as quart jugs and as hard as the grey-cream limestone of the house; and also another pear tree, very tall, by the church in the same town, the pears on it very early, small honey-pears coming in July, and then our own pears, the most magnificent Williams and Doyenne du Comice we ever saw, and trees of green-golden russets a little hard on the teeth; and finally the pears of those almost legendary orchards to which we drove on August and September afternoons and where we pocketed massive golden fallings while no one was looking and then tried to walk as if we hadn't a pair of pig's bladders in our trousers.

And also the colour of the leaves. With the fruit gone, in the last still days of October, the leaves of the pears used to turn green-orange, then almost pink, then copper and cherry in the sun. Then the first frost came. Finally they floated down and lay in the long grass under the tree like glowing shavings of walnut and mahogany, and were wet in the morning with dew.

VII

The New Country

PEARS and peaches, fuchsias and perpetual roses, penny plaice and golden sea poppy, terraces by the sea in the sun: whenever I think of them I think of the incomplete inscription on the gate on the Sussex Downs. It is right to die for one's country. But it is equally right to live for one's country and grow pears. One way or the other, it's no use getting sentimental now.

What are we going to do about it—the future: the future of the country? Whenever I come home on leave to the country I am struck by two things: first, and much more forcibly than a year ago, how little the country, the seasonal appearance and the colour and the feeling of it, changes in war; and secondly, and much more forcibly than a year ago, how little the people change. There is something significant as well as incongruous in these two notices on the Sussex Downs. Here too, in Kent, the notices about private property are still nailed up too permanently. The voice of the little property owner speaks against the cyclone of a world revolution: " But it's not right. They should have got permission from *me* before they broke in to move the incendiary bomb."

But it is not only here that I see the incongruous and the resistance to change. In London, which grows more and more like the unpleasant wen that Cobbett detested, I am invited by perhaps the most distinguished of all editors of periodicals on country life to lunch at the Farmers' Club. This delights me, and although it is war-time I look forward to simple country food, cooked in English country fashion. A Farmers' Club: why not farmers' food? Perhaps there will even be a regional dish or two. But after we have looked at the menu the editor and I look at each other. He is a man of more than seventy: twice my age. And now to all our common interests and reactions is added another. The menu is in French.

A year ago I walked with this same editor through his village in the Cotswolds. He had lived in the village for fifteen years; behind him lay a record of tireless attempts at reforms, housing and educational improvements, work on magisterial benches, county councils and committees. Though I was so much younger, we had all this and much more in common. We tried to look at the country as a whole, as an inseparable part of the whole English way of life, and not as a life separated and fenced off. To this ideal he had been dedicated, in much more selfless terms than myself, for as many years as I had lived. He had seen many changes, probably more good than bad. But I had a question: " Do you find you are any nearer the people ?"

I shan't forget his wife's despairing cry. " *Are* we any nearer ? Even after twenty years ?" she said. " Oh ! how well you know them, don't you ?"

" Yes," I said, " how well I know them."

" Does culture matter ?" says Mr E. M. Forster. " Cultivated people like you and me are a drop of ink in the ocean." We have only to substitute reform for culture and cultivated, and we have a question and answer that is equally true of the countryside. How many people care if the country tomorrow is different from the country today? In this morning's newspaper is the report, advocating a five-year plan for a better rural Britain, from the Scott Committee on Rural Land Utilisation. It is a very important report. How many people will give it a second thought? It is true that some people, perhaps an increasing number of people, care very much. But do the right people care? Some of them get confusedly and ardently religious about the country; they say incantations over compost heaps. Even a catalogue of fruit trees which we have, excellent in itself, is prefaced by a moral discourse on Man and his Maker. This brings us to the fact that yesterday, just when we needed it, we had a visit from our friend the fruit expert. As we talked to him we realised that our chapter on pears was not, after all, a trivial thing. Some things he said took us back to an article in the newspaper of last Sunday, in which an eminent educational authority was saying that it would of course be many many years before the benefits of a wider education were enjoyed by all.

Odd that we should begin with a light-hearted discussion on the fertility of Doyenne du Comice, and progress to reform, educational and otherwise, in the countryside. But gradually, as so often, the most irrelevant oddities became linked up: a walk in the Cotswolds, lunch at the Farmers' Club, an inscription on a Sussex gate, a newspaper article —they become part of the same pattern.

The fruit expert spends his life on a great Research Station. It is his job to experiment on grafting stocks, new methods of grafting, pruning, new varieties: in short, on the better production of fruit— and English fruit, especially English apples, nectarines and peaches, is the best in the world—in these islands. He told me in five minutes what was wrong with my fruit. Did I want apple trees for shade or for bearing fruit? Of all apples for a small garden I had planted, in Gascoyne's Scarlet and Blenheim, two of the worst. Both had scabbed badly and were constantly dying back. If I uprooted them I should have room for thirty cordons: ten or fifteen varieties in succession from July to Easter. In ten minutes he put the expert finish to a dream of years.

But this was not all. He had been to see, that day, several orchards: one, the best in Kent; another, belonging to a millionaire, quite the worst; another, next door to the best and belonging to one of those expensive schools for select young gentlemen, next but one to the worst; and another, ten or fifteen miles away and belonging to a young man of independent means, bad enough.

Four orchards, four men, an expert: how do they fit into the future? And the select young gentlemen? The millionaire, it was clear, did not really belong to the country: he was an absentee, engaged in important enterprises elsewhere, but contributing to the country the worst orchard, or the worst soil, in the worst situation in his county. The owner of the new Dotheboys Hall: he too was absent. More good land was wasted. Of the four, the fruit farmer, turning the soil to its fullest production, always experimenting, never too big to listen to the experts in research, alone had an economic place in the country-side. He alone, strictly, has a right to be there. And the young man of independent means had perhaps less right than any, and was the most interesting.

His orchard was bad; no doubt of that. It had once been good and could, with intelligence and care, be good again. Of its apples, the

Bramleys and Warners were still capable of large crops. There was, after all, as the expert pointed out, a war on, and it was as wrong to neglect an orchard, the source of fruit, as to neglect a shell factory, the source of defence, attack, destruction or survival or however you like to put it. Here were thirty acres of Kentish land not being rightly used in time of war. To some of us it seemed like a time of revolution. What was the young man going to do?

The young man, it seemed, was going to do nothing. Am I right in thinking that his reason for doing nothing was typical not only of the man, but the class, the generation and the education from which he had come? I hope not. The reason for his doing nothing was that he had no money.

By which he meant, apparently, that he had too few sources of independent means. Money, for him, meant something unearned. Living on the land, not by it or for it, he contributed nothing at all to the social community of which he was part. Also he was going to do nothing because, really, he did not understand trees and because, anyway, he did not believe in pruning. An expensive education, to repeat which for his children was apparently his chief concern, had taught him to regard land as a pleasant appendage to a house, a protection for a view and a convenient place to shoot over on summer evenings and winter afternoons.

This young man is not alone. He is part of a tradition: a tradition connected with the great house, the big estate, the park-like, man-made, man-preserved scenery everywhere. He too, like them, is affected by the revolution, towards which he is contributing little. The revolt is being waged by others, for many of whom he has a class contempt. He still dismisses servants with off-hand indifference, on the slightest pretext, turning them out of their cottages on the briefest possible notice, although the husbands and brothers of those same servants are in the revolt, fighting and perhaps dying in Libya, Malaya, on the sea, in the air or on the beaches of Dieppe. He has been brought up to regard humanity as divided into two classes, and not even three years of war have changed his view. To him the chief horror of war is that he has no money. It never occurs to him, apparently, to go out and, by the sweat of his hands, earn a little.

All about him the air is full of reforms for the countryside. They are put forward from the political angle, the social angle, even from the historical angle. We must have larger farms, says one; smaller farms, says another. We must stop the drift to the town: a drift that has, by the way, at least two hundred years' start on those who wish to stop it. We must produce more wheat and less milk; or more milk

and less wheat. Our salvation is in soil fertility; no, in distribution.
We need more smallholdings; we must abolish the rentiers. We must
revive handicrafts, oxen teams, and the maypole. On the contrary, we
need more tractors, more machinery, more electrification. We must
stop the loss of fertile land to indiscriminate building projects, the
figures of which are frightening. In the past forty years we have lost,
through city and town development, an area of farm land equal to
Bedfordshire and Buckinghamshire put together. In the effort to
change this, and much else, more words than ever before are being
written.

Only a fraction of these words, it seems to me, goes to the common
root of all the problems. And that common root is, and must always
be, the people. Our job is not to change the land, to revive or ex-
tinguish historical customs, to grow a predominance of this food or
that, but to change, if we can, the people. This means you, who read
this book, and I, who write it. It means the people of whom the wife
of the editor says: " Oh ! how well you know them !" It means the
young man with his bad orchard, his bad prejudices and his colossally
bad indifference to the land on which he idles away his life. It means
Mr Pimpkins. It means the lady who still, in the middle of a war that
is a revolution, advertises for " a housemaid and a cook: one other
maid kept; one lady." It means the millionaire absentee; the owner
of the expensive Dotheboys for young gentlemen; the politician who
never sees the villages of his constituency except at election time. It
means the villager who does not get on with the new people because
" they are Londoners and I never did get on with Londoners." It
means the Londoner who comes to the country for sleep and recrea-
tion. It means the clergyman who hasn't time to bother, and the
clergyman whose heart is broken because years of bothering have
brought no change. It means the clergyman's wife who can't be
bothered to make friends with the village, and the village which can't
be bothered to make friends with her. It means the farm labourer and
his wife; it means their sons who have learned to fly Spitfires and will
wonder, when they come home, if it is worth exchanging them for
pitchforks. It means the unknown person who scratches a Latin
inscription on a Sussex gate, and the unknown person who warns us
about the rights of private property. It means the major who writes
to the paper about the decline of fox hunting, and the colonel who, very
unexpectedly, is a Socialist. It means the schoolmistress and the child.

Above all, it means the schoolmistress and the child. For above
all, of course, it means education. Since we are to work in the countryside for the common good it is only right, it seems to me, that we should

start with common advantages. If we are to change the countryside it is reasonable to expect that we should, every one of us, be given the best means of changing it.

Until we get these means and these advantages we simply pile up about us a heap of abstract and confused ideals. We remain, you and I—the one of us who cares about country books and the other who writes them—the useless drop of ink in the ocean. We are identical with Mr Forster's cultivated people. There are too few of us, and alone we cannot change the rest. Yet the means of change is now, as always, education. Through new standards of it we shall free ourselves of the young gentleman with the useless orchard, the modern Mr Squeers, the indifferent villager, the indifferent clergyman, Mr Pimpkins and the rest. We shall get, if we want to get it enough, the new countryside.

The day after the fruit expert came to see us was very hot; the evening was calm and blue and humid over the cornfields. I had been reading that day, the last of my leave, a few pages of John Buchan, a writer I had not touched since schooldays, describing how, as a boy, he used to get up before dawn to fish in the burns of Scotland. Those charming pages suddenly incited me to do the same thing. I had never fished at dawn, a time always held to be the angler's paradise, but once I had written a story about it, a story of two very old men who also wanted to fish at dawn but who had somehow overslept and never got there. That night I slept rather poorly; it was warm and I was afraid of oversleeping. And in the dream an awful thing happened. I was fishing in a narrow place and got excited, and my rod, a forty-year-old Farlow given me very generously by a charming lady who also used to fish in Scottish waters, snapped off clean about three inches from the top. The tragedies of dreams are very real, and sometimes freeze their imagery on the mind. I woke about five o'clock, a bit confused and rather terrified at the freezing thought of breaking that rod, on which even a half-pound fish feels as if it were straining in the socket of a catapult. "Should I go?" I said; and my wife said: "Of course you should go. It will be lovely for you. It will do you good." Women are, I notice, always mildly restrained about fishing. They make you feel a little apologetic about it. So that sooner or later one of you ends by saying that you think it will do you good.

I got out of bed at last and made myself a cup of tea in the kitchen, mixing a ball of paste while the kettle boiled. The dew was like frost on the grass; the sun was not quite above the grey-mauve clouds, and the night-scented stocks were still open wide. I got on my bicycle

*A flock of wild duck clattered
fussily up from the reeds.*

and rode off to the lake, taking in the very pure, rather cold air in deep breaths. As I rode down the hill there seemed no one but me in the world. In the wheatfield by the lake the corn-ears were shining with dew and looked the colour of brandy-snaps. There was dew everywhere by the lakeside. A shining tide of it had broken over the high blonde grasses, never cut all summer, and it was so heavy on the green bunches of elderberry that they hung down and touched the grass tips. The long light purple heads of loosestrife and the creamy puffs of meadow sweet were drenched by it to a slightly duller colour than they would be when dried in the sun.

As I walked up by the water, under the alders and past the quince trees, where the fruits were about as big as small honey pears, the first siren of the day began wailing across the fields, followed by another and another, until there were four or five sounding together. By the time I was getting my rod together under the chestnut trees on the river bank all of them had ceased and it was deadly quiet again. It was still cool and I could feel the dew cool on my feet where it had soaked already through my shoes. The fish were rising and plopping under the trees as they do in the late evenings. I then made the discovery that I had left my worms on the kitchen table, and I dismally remembered that last time I had come fishing worms had been the only successful bait.

Sure enough, I fished all up the river and got nothing but those nibbling and bobbling bites that come of paste and tiddlers. But the day was wonderful. The sun was coming up and spreading a sort of butteriness on the water, the meadows and the corn beyond. A flock of wild duck clattered fussily up from the reeds at the western end of the lake, the same place where I had seen not long before two herons waiting for fish, standing on one leg, as wooden and immobile as if set down there out of glass cases.

I climbed the fence and walked up into the meadow, away from the trees, into full sun. Up the river stood the two churches, square, simple, each on a hill. The big water-mill, once white, now grey as a battleship, was just visible beyond the bridge. On the far bank stood the mansion, pink and green, shining magnolias by its porch, cedars spreading layers of black shadow on the grass: another great house in decay, part of the revolution, its lovely rooms filled with officers and men. At one time the stable clock used to strike every quarter with rather a brief and brittle tone that cut across the shallow valley, but it is evidently out of order now. In one of the few gaps in the trees along the river bank where the mansion can be seen a clump of bright yellow monkey-musk flowered in the mud: sometimes, I think, the loveliest of water flowers, the yellow of the trumpets so water-pure and clear in the first morning sun.

It was now half-past six, and no fish at all. I knew that any moment now I should drop my paste, step on it, and spend twenty minutes looking for it before going disconsolately home. There were no caddis-grubs, and there was nothing for it but to dig worms if I could find a place to dig and something to dig with. Finally I found an oak stick and a patch of wet ground, and I dug up half a dozen very anæmic worms which looked as if they wouldn't tempt a gudgeon.

I put them into my pocket and went up to my favourite pool, where the water is black and deep and the swim from the bend in the stream goes slowly round in swinging circles under the alder trees. I put on a worm and made a gentle cast between the overhanging branches. An hour's discouragement with paste had made me careless. I made the cast and looked away. I looked back again just in time to see the float shooting away like a scarlet arrow down to the depths of the pool. It was too late, of course, and I missed the strike. But I cast straight back again, with half the nibbled worm still on the hook, and the float dived down again. The half-pound roach made a fuss that would not have disgraced, if all the fishing stories one hears are true, a two-pound trout. I put in again, and the same thing happened. This time the rod bent like a whip, and for two seconds there was no moving or holding what was on the end. The smallness of the resulting roach, again about half a pound, quite astounded me. Two more roach in ten minutes, the last just under the pound, made the same fierce circles of protest across the pool.

And then something happened. As I took the last fish off the hook, the rod unexpectedly whipped back and the line skipped into a tangle in the tip. A little carelessly I pulled down the line, and in a second the dream of the night, frozen on my mind, became a reality. The rod snapped exactly as it had done in the dream, three inches from the tip, filling me with the same frozen dismay.

I went home then; the day is done when the rod breaks. And already the day seemed old to me. The touch of coolness had gone and the air was as warm as new bread. At home the kittens ate the fish, crunching the raw scales as children crunch acid drops, and I ate my breakfast, feeling that slight self-importance that you do feel when you have been out with the dawn, hours before other people.

In a few hours I started west. The day was hot now; the heat lay bright and scorching across the corn of the Sussex Weald. At Brighton the sun was slapped on to the Regency stucco with southern brilliance, and you could feel all the summer pouring down, like the light through

67

a burning-glass, through the mid-afternoon of a single August day.
Up the Channel, going east, went a line of small naval craft, slightly
larger than corvettes, and there was a little gunfire, like thunder shaken
out of the haze over France. What was happening? There was
something in the air. The feeling of tension that hangs about the sea,
the sense of fatality, the sense of the air being charged with destiny on
hot and glassy afternoons and with foreboding on grey evenings when
the yellow western light is chilly and savage on the ripped crests of the
waves, was making itself felt that afternoon. As I left Brighton and
went west it increased.

But I had grown used to scares, and took no notice. Arundel was
sleepy and majestic and calm in the falling evening light. It looked
all that England should look: implacable, decent, imperishable, touched
with tender light. A few old men were leaning over the river parapet,
watching the yellow water go down to the sea. In an hour a few pilots,
always more hilarious here than elsewhere, would be shaking the
complacency of the pleasant Norfolk bar. The Castle, into which
Cromwell's men had lobbed cannon balls from the ramparts by the
church, now looked as indestructible as a mountain.

I drove on into Chichester, on the atmosphere and inhabitants of
which W. H. Hudson once delivered an aggressively jaundiced attack,
and which I should now like to counteract by saying that the people
of Chichester were, in the summer of 1942, all that people should be in
their conduct to a stranger. I was never in a town where the inhabitants
gave more charm and courtesy or plain decent friendliness of heart.
Whether you drank milk punch in The Punch Bowl or ate the excellent
dinner in the rather austere and beautiful Dolphin, whether you bought
a pair of pyjamas or a necklace or a dozen frames for the beehives or
only a postage stamp, you got more courtesy and ordinary honest
humanity in Chichester than you would ever get in London in a month
of Sundays. In that small, Roman-patterned cathedral town, with
its pleasant eighteenth-century by-ways and its sun-lit garden walls
creamed over in high summer with Alberic Barbier roses in the walks
behind the cathedral, there was a warmth of heart as right as the red
walls of the houses. You felt the real gentleness of the south there.

The people of Chichester had seen, like the people of so many mild
and sleepy towns in Southern England, the greatest sky battles of history.
To the neighbouring aerodromes they had given some of the adulation,
in the summer of 1940, that towns give in peace-time to their football
teams. They recorded the score of fallen aircraft in communicative
placards hung behind their saloon bars. " Bless 'em all," the placards
said, and they expressed, through those simple words, the regional

pride in a national triumph.   The war has come very near to the people of Southern England and it has, I think, changed them.   They live as it were with their heads up, alert.   The complacency which descended on many districts of Midland and Northern England and settled there and became as thick as the pile of an expensive carpet never had a chance to settle in the South.   From Chichester you can see the sea.   From the sea rises that air of foreboding that may, any fine summer day, break into the scarlet splinters of another battle.

That evening I drove out of Chichester, and was flagged on the way by an excited American soldier with an accent as ripe and furry and southern as the skin of a peach.   " Sur," he called me.   " Sur, could you drive me back ? "   He was excited because all Americans had been recalled to camp, but I was cold and had been in the war three years, and nothing could excite me now.   On the way we passed many American soldiers, pedalling bicycles as if they hoped to get to Moscow that night, and as we passed them the American leaned out of the window with ripe scorn.   " Pedal, you carpet baggers ! " And then to me: " I'm from South Carolina, sur.   Still fighting the Civil War, you see."

" You like the summer now it's come ? " I said.   " We've had two days of it.   Or does it bother you ? "

" I don't care about the summer, sur," he said.   " But heck, I'd like a beef-steak."

" I seem to have heard that before," I said.

I set him down at the cross-roads where he branched off for his camp, and he almost fell out of the car in his eagerness to get out on to the chalky road leading to the hills.   I put on the act of a man tired with three years of war, and smiled.

Everywhere the corn was ripe and the smell of the corn blew in at the open windows of the car.   Had the moon been so deep and mellow over the Virginian corn in 1862 ?   The Civil War was not over and, since it was incidentally if not primarily a clash of ideologies, never would be.   The eagerness of the young man from Carolina falling out on to an English road between fields of English corn in the naïve belief that the invasion of France was about to begin that night might well have been the eagerness of a young man going to fight for General Lee.

In the Mess there was a curious atmosphere of muddle.   I could see no one I knew, and wondered why, so early, everyone had gone to bed.   There was no one to talk to and the blasphemous, careless air of the middle summer had gone.   It was like returning to school long after you had left and finding no longer the gilt of the golden days.

I went to bed and forgot immediately the young American, the

Civil War, the naval craft steaming steadily up the Channel. And in the late hours of the night the invasion of Dieppe began.

All through that day I had a sense of being isolated from that raid. I ate and talked with the men who flew in it, heard their stories, saw the wonderful child-like light on the face of a pilot who, dressed in enormous white sweater and trousers, had been picked out of the sea. All the time I thought of Dieppe. It was the Dieppe that Sickert had painted, and in which I, with my wife, had once stayed during a summer in the early thirties. I remembered the *pension* where the regulars made the ten-franc bottle of Graves last the week, and when we too looked at every penny and spent the days idling in the sun. I remembered trivial details like the beautiful cakes in a white *pâtisserie*, glimpses of gardens through iron gateways on the steep streets outside the town. I remembered the mornings and the smell of coffee and the market women in the streets with their small cheap peaches, their ducks tied to their legs, and their baskets of sun-yellow butter. It was all now as remote as the Civil War : perhaps remoter.

It was not until the next afternoon that I got another picture of Dieppe. Beyond Arundel a young Canadian flagged the car. Would I take him to L——? he said. He wanted to find out how many of his friends were alive.

" And what was it like ?" I said.

" Hell, sur," he said. " Just plain hell."

" Just that ?" I said.

" Just that, sur," he said. " Just a wee bit worse than Dunkirk."

As we drove along, the golden memory of Dieppe, my own memory, faded. It grew red with blood. " Don't think I'm yellow, sur," the Canadian said. " Don't think I'm yellow. But I don't want it again."

As he talked I remembered seeing in a bookshop that day a book with one of those glamorous Shakespearean titles we are too fond of quoting in times of war. " Went the day well ?" it asked, and now the answer was: " No, the day was bloody, the day was just plain hell."

Before I said goodbye to the Canadian there was a new picture of Dieppe in my mind. It glowed with one odd little incident. At the height of battle, when the beaches were like a slaughter-house floor and some of the tanks were bogged and the tracer was like a red-hot curtain of flying beads, an old Frenchman, a man of sixty-five or so, proceeded to bicycle along the promenade. Whether in defiance or stupidity no one seemed to know. But of all the stories of the Dieppe raid I should like to hear, most of all, the story of that bicycling Frenchman making his stupid or courageous, indifferent or determined, oblivious or predestined way along the quay, somehow without catastrophe, between the curtains of English and German fire. Of all the stories, that is either the craziest or the greatest. It is possible to read in it some of that intensely national contempt which the French, a nation perhaps even more insular than ourselves, have for other nations. They ask for neither the English, whom they do not understand, nor the Germans, whom they hate. They ask only to be French, and to be left to bicycle between us, alone.

So I came back to Kent in the late afternoon. Once again I looked at the country: the corn, the reddening apples, the hops thick as forests on the poles. As I looked at the rich and changeless countryside I thought of the young man from Carolina, still fighting the Civil War, the young Canadian, who had been on a day trip to Dieppe and had seen a France more violently coloured than Gauguin could have painted it, and the old Frenchman bicycling, for God alone knew what reason, along the promenade of no-man's-land.

I thought also of the young man with the orchard: not believing in pruning because he did not understand it, not understanding because he did not care. I thought of him with his thirty acres of rich Kent land in decay, his notion that money gave privilege, his deliberate isolation from the world in which so many of us, out of common stupidities or common mistakes or common ideals, were blundering forward towards, we hoped, a more decent daylight. I thought of his arrogance and his gigantic indifference in what Hardy called the Time of the Breaking of Nations.

That day the nations had been broken a little more, and on the beaches of Dieppe someone had been killed. But it was not the young man from Carolina, leaping as eagerly out of the car as if he were about to fight for Robert Lee, or the young Canadian whose fear was that you might think him afraid, or the old Frenchman bicycling with inscrutable purpose between the catastrophic fire of two foreign armies. It was not the English pilot picked out of the sea.

It was, though he did not know it, the young man with the orchard. And I for one am glad that he is dead.

VIII

The Old Tradition

"YES," said the famous writer on agriculture, as we sat talking in London, "he is dead. Win, lose or draw, he and his class are dead. They know they are dead. They did not want the war because they knew they would be dead if it came."

So they too, it seemed, had died for their country. For in war it is a curious thing that it is not only the fighters who die, but those who stay at home. It is not only men who perish, but institutions. In the last war we saw the Church, the great house, and the village community disintegrate and lose their power and character as if it were they who had been the direct objectives of the war. In this war we see the great house, now taken over by young men whose war is in the air, slip a little farther into decay. We see the Church floundering a little deeper into the lonely marshes of abstract ideals: planless, directionless, out of touch. Confused between Christianity and organised religion, it writes its bewildered letters to the press, asking where faith has gone. It inducts its parsons in villages that do not need them. There are, I think, six hundred of them in Kent alone, not counting Catholics and

Nonconformists, and sometimes I wonder at their purpose. Sometimes, perhaps very often, they must wonder themselves. For they too, in this war, are dying for their country, and of all the relics of the old country-side one is sorriest for them. They draw their life from an impossible system that seems to have no sane place in the planning of the future. Their lives were once clear and, I think, decent and useful. They had something to give which could not be given otherwise. They supplied education of a kind, advice, direction, a link between man and master. Where are they now? They are condemned to an impossible life in impossible houses. I think of the huge rectory of my own village: built for some reason of cold yellow Fenland brick in a district of warm stone and warmer brick and tile. It must have been hideous when built. Time has made it more hideous still. It has fifteen rooms, not to speak of an entrance hall into which you could literally drive a hearse and four horses, a job for which the whole atmosphere of the house seems admirably fitted. It has no electric light. To heat the hall alone you need a colossal stove which even then, in bad winters, does not keep the temperature more than a point or two above freezing. The plan of the house is based on the notion that servants are four a penny and have the strength of oxen. The atmosphere of it seems to indicate that the incumbents are all ascetics and celibates and have the mental fortitude of monastics trained on hair shirts and self-denial. The garden is rich and charming if you can somehow afford four gardeners and you have the capacity to eat a ton of vegetables and fruit a year. As a nursing home for the aged and blind, a country lunatic asylum or an isolation hospital for virulent infections, it might be admirable. As a home it is the equivalent of asking every parson and his wife to spend their lives in a dungeon. It is in fact a great wonder to me that the suicide rate among country parsons is not higher than it is.

I once made these points in an article in a periodical. The resulting correspondence, mostly from parsons' wives, showed not only how close to reality my remarks were, but how glad—how pathetically glad— the clergy themselves were that at last someone had spoken for them. One could only wonder at their own incapacity for revolt. They seemed to stand with shoulders bowed, without hope. " How long we have waited for someone to say a word for us!" they said. Why hadn't they said it themselves? They were part of a dying system and yet had no capacity, apparently, to diagnose the disease. One is sorry for them, living in their impossible dungeons in a world that has outgrown their usefulness—but for them, as for so much else that decays in the countryside, it's no use getting sentimental now.

No; they too are dying, and if there is to be a rural Utopia after the

73

war they, as far as one can see, will have little part in it. But is there to be a Utopia, and above all do we want one? The English, I think, are not very good at Utopias, which argue perfection, lotus-eating, and eternal sunlight. We are not very good at perfection; we are no lotus-eaters; and we should never endure, in a country where all the tender and cloudy charm of the landscape comes from rain, eternal sunlight. If you gave the English a Utopia tomorrow they would never rest until they had remoulded it nearer to their own cranky heart's desire. We are a very restless people, showing to the world a very deceptive complacency. We are fond of change, and at the same time like stability. Notice the English attitude to weather. After three weeks of unbroken sun we cry out for rain, and the relief in the air is immense when it comes. Give us three weeks of snow, a rare occurrence with us, and we are depressed for the sight of grass. Give us rain after drought and in three days we are crying for sun again. We thrive on change and on the knowledge that that change will have a constant part in our lives.

Somehow, out of this need for change and the reverence for stability, has grown what we call the English tradition. What is this tradition? How can we explain it, for example, to a foreigner? The outside world constantly wonders about England—so very small, yet so very powerful. It thinks of it as a powerful industrial island, radiating commerce. It recognises its reputation for solidity—what has been called English backbone. It remembers how the industry of the world was revolutionised by inventions in that island—the steam engine, for example, and the power loom. It remembers England as the pioneer and creator of great ships. It thinks of English manufacture, English oak, English iron and steel, and now English aeroplanes. All these are the concrete evidence of English power as seen by the outside world.

Yet something else lies behind these things. What is it? I suggest that it has something to do with the genius of English hands, and a great deal to do with the receptivity, the plasticity, of English character. Somewhere behind the great riveting yards of the ship-builders, behind the assembly lines crowded with Spitfires, behind the steel span of bridges in Australia and Africa and the steel tracks of railways all over the world, there stand generations of English craftsmen whose work has been shaped by the exceptional testing standards which now make English products synonymous with strength and durability. Working with hammer and iron, needle and thread, lathe and tree, cotton and pillows, these craftsmen are some of the obscure but vital motive forces behind the power of a small island. They are the little things which influence and shape the great.

A roof designed to endure for perhaps a thousand years.

All through England, in country districts especially, you can still see examples of this traditional craftsmanship: things which have been standing up against time, war, change and, not least, the English climate, for hundreds of years and which are for ever part of the standard of English values. Look, for example, at the picture of the English timbered barn-roof. It is beautiful; it is a magnificent example of strength and craft. But it is also reminiscent of something. You see at once that it is like the upturned frame of a ship. It has the same essential strength and grace and power of a ship that must be built to sail out to discovery on unfriendly seas. Between the men who built that roof and the men who build ships in English shipyards today there is an invisible but unbroken link. Their standards of test are the same, and it is not fantastic to suggest that the ships are powerful partly because, centuries ago, English carpenters made a roof designed to endure for perhaps a thousand years.

Or look at the picture of the church spire. There are hundreds like it in the green countryside of England: slender, delicate, yet designed with such strength and balance that they have been withstanding English rain and gale and blizzard for nearly a thousand years. They also are reminiscent of something. The clear clean line, so delicate and yet strong, is near to what we now call streamlined. It is very close in beauty and cleanness and functional strength to the line of a modern aeroplane. It has something of the appearance of an object poised in flight.

Or take a traditional English bed-quilt. It is an example of a different kind of strength. It does not recall ships or aeroplanes; there is nothing of the modern functional world to which we can attach it for comparison. Its strength is in its pattern and the special character of the hands that worked it. The hands that worked it are probably the hands of miners' wives: women from the raw industrial district of Durham in the north, where life is hard and grim and dirty and without visible poetry. Yet the pattern of this quilt has not changed in a single detail for 400 years; all that time the beautiful glowing design of tulips and roses has been handed from generation to generation. But there is more in it than this. For the design that is worked unchanged today by the wives of miners is the original design worked by a royal Tudor household. It was once the exclusive prerogative of English queens. Yet after 400 years, handed down not only from generation to generation but from royalty to nobility, from nobility to aristocracy, from aristocracy to the very poor, it retains, unbroken and untouched, every detail of its original delicate line. Its strength is the strength of common inheritance.

But there is something else. Though so beautiful in design, this quilt is made for use. In winter, on the north-east coast of England, it is bitterly cold. So the quilt must be warm, and its delicate and carefully preserved design is really only an afterthought. The first and great test for the quilt, as for the church spire, the ship, the roof, the railway and the bridge, is utility. It is the test which above all guides and pleases the Englishman.

Take again an English farm wagon. It is a vehicle of utility. Its chief purpose is to carry the summer hay from the meadows and later the sheaves of wheat, oats and barley from the harvest fields. Would it not be simple, and quite adequate, to have a plain, strong design that would be common to any district in England? Undoubtedly it would. Why, then, is it rather delicately and sparsely built? Again, it looks rather like a ship, something like a galleon on wheels. It is scrolled and painted, like the design of the body varies from one county to another, sometimes several times within each county. This is English individuality: the hatred of regimentation and loss of independence, making itself felt even in the wagons of the fields. And why are they so slight to look at, so pared down? It is because they are built of heavy English woods—the famous oak, the strong white ash, the dark earth-coloured elm. A wagon built solidly of such woods would be in itself a hard load for a horse to pull. So from each wheel-spoke, each shaft, from every corner and line of the body, a little wood has been pared away. Every piece so cut away means an ounce less for the horse to pull. The final result is a new lightness in the whole design—a beauty created, as the English craftsman so often creates it, by the rules of utility.

It would, however, be a mistake to carry this too far. For the English may frequently be found loving decoration for its own sake. Consider the fantastic luscious carved fruit often found on church screens, the mural design on houses, the fox and hounds making an inn sign that runs over the road. They are examples of another side of English craftsmanship, of English temperament breaking into poetry. Do not believe, in fact, the popular conception of the Englishman: phlegmatic, insular, slow to change, solid, unimaginative. The range of the English temperament is very wide; it is capable of expression in great strength, but also in great delicacy; it is invincibly solid but also infinitely elastic. The temperament that is capable of beating the racing little fox and dogs out of iron for an inn sign is capable also of the majesty of the great university church, King's College Chapel, at Cambridge. The genius that shapes the curves of the Forth Bridge

77

can be capable of the strong, simple curves of the thatched roof, exhibiting the same strength and poetry on a cottage of the tiniest country village.

We are, in fact, a very contradictory people. We hide one part of ourselves by another. We are an agricultural people industrialised in the last 150 years, and it is significant that our greatest revolution is that created by the machine against the soil. It is still more significant that it still goes on. Centuries of tradition, born out of contact with the earth, now impose themselves on a generation of steel and iron, bakelite and aluminium, tank and plane, battleship and micrometer. Behind us lie the centuries of test. From this test there emerge and survive the things we now regard naturally as part of our traditional inheritance. Through this test, for example, we chose oak as the national wood, though it was not indigenous, so that today it is famous everywhere as a symbol of English toughness and imperishability. Out of it we made the hammer-beam roofs that sheltered us, the pews where we went to pray, the bastion gates of castles, the floors of the smallest cottage, and, above all, the ships in which we went on voyages of discovery everywhere.

But consider, finally, a simple flock of sheep, and by means of it you can learn something odd about English temperament and tradition. You can learn that that temperament and that tradition are plastic, infinitely adaptable things. Sheep have been kept as domestic animals by men for thousands of years. They have been kept by Englishmen for centuries, and because the English climate is damp and mild and English fields eternally green, sheep have played a great part in English life.

Today, as in 1572, refugees in thousands have come from a persecuted continent to England. In 1572 they brought with them the art of lace making, and taught it so well that nearly 400 years later it is still being made. Today Czechs and Rumanians are doing something with sheep that Englishmen have never done. They are teaching English farmers to milk them. From that milk the English farmer is being taught to make a new kind of cheese by refugees, just as English women were being taught 400 years ago to make a new kind of lace. In time the lace became part of our tradition; so, too, may the cheese.

This may be a little thing, but it is also significant. We are an island people, but we are not isolated or insular. From this island much goes out, but much also comes in. It is the rain of the Atlantic that keeps our fields eternally green, and in the same way the ideas and art of other peoples, often persecuted peoples, have for centuries permeated our tradition and kept it living. That tradition, tough as oak but fine as lace, imperishable as stone but buoyant as a ship, old but infinitely classic, in turn goes out and becomes part of the culture of the world. It is this that will not die.

IX

The Green Hedges

WE think of the green fields, too, as imperishable. They, too, are part of us. I was born among the pastures: on that large East Midland plain that takes in Northamptonshire and its nine adjoining counties, Buckinghamshire, Oxfordshire, Warwickshire, Bedfordshire, Lincolnshire, Huntingdonshire, Leicestershire, Cambridgeshire and the smallest and perhaps the best of them all, the dillin pig of the litter, Rutland. As it also takes in Essex and Hertfordshire, and parts of Yorkshire and Nottinghamshire and Worcestershire and most of Norfolk and Suffolk, it must be reckoned the largest plain in England. If you reckon it in terms of impressive landscape features it is probably also the dullest plain in England. Its hills, until you come to the boundaries of the Chilterns in the south, the Cotswolds in the south-west, and the real hills of Nottinghamshire and Derbyshire in the north, are not much more than bumps made by generations of gnats on the green skin of the land. It contains no natural lakes until you reach the Broads almost on the seacoast to the eastward; it contains the remnants of half a dozen forests, but in countries other than England they would probably be reckoned as copses. Its only true and permanent natural features are its rivers, and it is in reality five river plains—six if you include the Humber—in one: the Ouse, the Nene, the Welland and the Trent flowing out to the east, the Avon down to the west. Judged by the standards of Devon and Somerset, the Yorkshire hills and dales, and the magnificence of Cumberland and Westmorland, and the hills of Gloucestershire and Derbyshire which make its boundaries, it has nothing to offer. When I compare it with Kent and Sussex, in which most of my life is now spent, I see it as a country without richness and without any great variety of scene and colour. In my mind's eye I see it as the greenest piece of England, which it probably is, and for some reason the most orderly. It lacks that enchanting disorder of deep-bellied hills, thick woods, sly lanes, rich coloured villages and luxuriant hop-gardens which is the south country. It is a pattern of sobriety. Against the southern plain, the great weald running from the North Downs to the South, with which I propose to compare it, it is like the homely girl compared with the beauty, the plain oak trouser-polished chair-seat compared with the mahogany Chippendale, the suet pudding compared with the trifle. Yet, as I hope to show, this plain homely pudding pattern of elm and grass and hedges is the basis on which the entire English countryside is built. It is the very thing which makes the English country what it is: something different from any other country in the world.

For more than twenty years I felt myself to have been unlucky in having been brought up in such country. I spent a childhood unconsciously entranced by it, magnifying dribbling little brooks to the brave beauty of torrents, tiny nightingale copses to the deep luxuriance of woods. I grew up to know the ash and the elm and the willow better than any other tree because they were the staple trees of the landscape, and to know hardly any other type of field than pasture and the massive ploughed parallels of steel clay that would later be roots and corn. I knew no other hedgerow, except the rule-straight line of laid hawthorn or the high cow-rubbed umbrella-shaped variation of it that is, as W. H. Hudson once pointed out, one of the greater glories of the English landscape. But it was only natural as time went on that I should grow tired of a landscape in which a beech tree was a rarity, in which elder or sweet-chestnut were never seen, and in which fields and copses were giving way more and more to raw Edwardian villas, rows of workers' cottages and an occasional factory. At twenty I disliked the Midlands; at twenty-five I hated them; at thirty, having left them, I began to understand them. I began to see how fortunate I had been to have been brought up on that diet of clay pudding which is as fundamental to English scenery as Yorkshire pudding is to English dietary.

I feel that I was fortunate for this reason. A man brought up in Devon or the dales of Yorkshire or the Westmorland lake country is often found never to have any real taste in other scenery. He has been brought up too well; he has never known what it is to be poor. Whereas a man brought up on a flat plain diet, as I myself was, has a taste capable of being educated in any kind of scenery. For him Exmoor and Dovedale and Windermere are pure caviare; the North Downs and the Malvern Hills and the Cotswolds are piled dishes of fruit. Poverty has given him perspective. Again, fine scenery makes a man proud and jealous. To a Westmorland man there is nothing like his native hills and waters; to a Devonian there is nothing like Devon; and all the world knows what a Yorkshireman thinks of Yorkshire. These men are as proud and jealous of their native muckles as high-coloured cocks. In the final estimate of grandeur there is nothing in the world that can beat their own. They can never say, and never would if they could, " This reminds me of Derwentwater," or, more unthinkable still, " This is as good as Yorkshire." But the man brought up on the plain-pudding country is decently humble, knowing there are places much better than his own; he knows, too, that there are places just like his own. The only time I went to Cheshire I saw the Midland countryside repeated exactly in the Cheshire plain, and I got from it a sense of friendliness and comfort. As I drive through the flattest parts of Somerset I see a countryside of willow and osier, elm and grassland, that in its unexotic ordinariness might be any part of a dozen homely counties. The same goes for the eastern parts of Yorkshire, though every Yorkshireman will probably call it an insult, for much of Worcestershire and Berkshire and, in fact, for odd un-expected bits of every county in England. It should never be for-gotten that most of the English countryside as we see it today is man-made; and that the part most completely shaped by man is this plain, fundamental chequerwork of flat field and hedgerow. And in one sense this is the only part which matters. It is the thing which nourishes the community, without which England would be poverty-stricken. It is essentially utilitarian; yet it provides exactly those pictures of which Englishmen in foreign countries are supposedly reminded at homesick moments, and which foreigners take away with them and cannot get over: the tranquil, orderly, park-like greenness, hedges of hawthorn in bloom, cattle grazing in deep meadows, sheep folded in pastures as short and green as lawns. In America, for example, they have a million square miles of countryside which will knock even Yorkshire into a cocked hat; in the State of Minnesota alone they claim ten thousand lakes; and in New Hampshire you may drive for hundreds of miles through country as rich and glorious as Devon and Somerset and the English county from which the state gets its name. But the country they cannot repeat and for which all Englishmen are deeply and honestly envied is the county about which I am writing. This, to them, is the real England.

It would be a mistake, I think, to argue that it is the real England: to the exclusion, that is, of all other parts. In praising England it is a fatal thing to extol one bit over another. For another remarkable thing about English scenery is its capacity for variation in a small space. If you travel across the plain of Lombardy from Milan to Venice you see exactly the same flat, dike-crossed, willow-spiked countryside for something like five hours. It is not possible to do such a thing in England for five minutes. To speak of Northampton-shire as if it were an elongated shape of pasture decorated into shapes of hawthorn hedges for the whole of its area would be absurd. From its north-eastern end, where its hawthorn hedges are giving way at last to low stone walls and an accompanying feeling of space and sturdy dignity, down to its south-western end, where the walls are beginning again and the land is rising like bare folds of dough towards the Cotswolds, it can produce a dozen tricks of change, though the funda-mentals remain the same. This is true of all its neighbours, of all their neighbours in turn. They each have the same infinite capacity not only for variation in beauty, but also in ugliness. There is a twenty-mile strip of Northamptonshire, five miles wide, running from the Bedfordshire border to Leicestershire, where it is possible to see how badly man-made landscape withstands the final attack of man and machine. The towns, once villages of golden and russet ironstone, crowned by the most magnificent church spires in England, are like gawky, raw-limbed boys that have outgrown their first long trousers. They are neither one thing nor another, neither town nor village, neither new nor old. Red brick has broken out like a rash among the sheep-coloured and russet walls and houses of local stone, with which nobody builds any longer. The factories are harsh red scabs on the slopes of the river valleys. They do not belong there. They have made a plain, homely country into depressing half-rural, half-urban slums of industry.

The moment you step off this strip of industrial development you begin to see the East Midland plain at its best. No writing on the English countryside is complete without a reference to the architecture, and here, from Higham Ferrers on the Nene up through Oundle and

Stamford and over the border into the toy hilly-hollows of Rutland, it is the architecture rather than the land which enchants. It stands as naturally on the landscape, the soft grey limestone interspersed with odd corners and patterns of gold-brown ironstone, as a flock of sheep in which there is a sprinkling of brown. This stone is exactly right for the soft undulation and calm colours of the land. It is a superb instance of nature providing on the spot exactly the right medium for man's activities; and it seems to me beyond doubt that if man had gone on using this limestone, decorating it with deeper tone-patterns of iron, this piece of the Midland plain running out of Northamptonshire into the whole of Rutland would have been as architecturally famous, perhaps more famous, than the Cotswolds themselves. But much of what was done, and done largely up to the eighteenth century, still remains. The square at Higham Ferrers, the whole of Oundle, almost the whole of Stamford, are all completely entrancing. But if Stamford stands with Cirencester as a perfect example of the English stone-built town at its best, the villages for twenty miles round are as absolutely satisfying and sound and beautiful as the names themselves: Rockingham, overlooking the entirely green Welland plain; Uppingham; Fotheringhay, with a superb church standing like a small lost cathedral over the graves of kings; Elton; Deene; Colly Weston, which gives the stone tiles that are one of the best features of the whole district; Kingscliffe; Weldon, giving the famous creamy stone; Lilford, with a mansion and a stone humpbacked bridge over the Nene that is not equalled anywhere in England; Caldecott; Oakham, the silly, one-eyed, one-policeman, charming county town of Rutland; and last, and probably best of all, Apethorpe. For every thousand eulogies of what are to me the much overrated villages of Devon, you will not see a single mention of Apethorpe. Yet Apethorpe is the last word in villages planned and governed and preserved by and according to the standards of the great house. If all examples of rural dictatorship could produce results like Apethorpe, then I would vote for a wholesale return to the principles of the Victorian squirearchy. This village does not contain a single house out of keeping with the enormous pale stone mansion standing behind its stout defences of woodland. It is the perfect thing. It has little of the picture-page picturesqueness of villages which seem to have been made exclusively for photographers and tourists; it is simply something that has been made, honestly and reverently, out of the stone of the district, primarily for use, secondarily but triumphantly for beauty. Its soft handful of straight-cut stone is a magnificent example of what the English system of squire dictatorship could do at its best. It is not bettered anywhere in England.

A superb church standing like a small lost cathedral over the graves of kings.

I have not mentioned this stone architecture, remarkable and lovely though it is, simply for the purpose of dilating on something beautiful. I would like to go on talking of it, in its humblest and sturdiest in the stone walls which replace the hedges, at its most splendid in the mansions: Kirby Hall, Deene, Burghley House, Lilford, Castle Ashby, Drayton House, Lyveden New Building, Apethorpe, and the famous spired churches. But this is only one bit of the green pudding country, a thumb-nail fraction of all England. The purpose of mentioning it is really to go on and compare it with something else. For it is obvious that the land, this kind of land more than any other, is nothing without the architecture, and it seems to me that the architecture of the pudding country is often far more remarkable than that of most impressive districts. It is as though the inhabitants of a plain and ordinary countryside felt a lack of any specially striking beauty in the landscape and built impressively or decoratively in order to make up for it. In the almost too rich countryside of Devon, for example, the greater part of the architecture will not bear talking about; it has the un-inspired carelessness of a self-satisfied people. Whereas on the really flat, and to some people depressing, plain of Huntingdonshire and Cambridgeshire the architecture, though humble, shows many signs of being in the hands of a dissatisfied and urgently restless people. The people of the warm, damp honey valleys of Devon carry on no struggle with nature; life is extremely and perhaps dangerously soft. But the people of the Fens and the outer Fen districts keep up a constant struggle; they are continually at war with sea winds, an unhealthy countryside and incursions of flood and sea. The whole ground under their feet is artificially guarded against disaster. Such a people might easily be excused for taking no interest in what their houses looked like. Yet a continual struggle against adversity and the oppressive fact of living on a drab and totally flat surface have heightened both their need for colour and their determination to secure it. Thus the cottage architecture of the extreme eastern section of the Midland plain, over a wide area of Bedfordshire, Huntingdonshire and Cam-bridgeshire, is almost exotically colour-washed. Cream and white are not enough for these people; they must have yellow and orange, beery shades of brown, deepest terra-cotta, crushed strawberry pink, the blue of blue-bags, an occasional fling in flamboyant red, a wash of startling emerald. In such a village as Kimbolton, a model of well-preserved rural quietness, a village in a thousand, the short, beautifully kept main street might be the home of a collection of irresponsible house painters. It glows with orange and white and brown and green and black, one of the most extraordinary and lovely streets in England.

And it is worth noting that England is not the only country in which such a desire for colour is shown by plain dwellers: the landscape of Holland is full of houses similarly coloured, so in less degree is the plain of Lombardy, and so, as a glance at the pictures of Van Gogh will show, are the plains of Southern France.

But arguments about the country have a way of not completing themselves. The flat country of Hertfordshire, the southern end of the plain, ought to oblige me by producing a remarkable architecture in stone or paint embellishments. But it doesn't. It produces something quite sober. Perhaps, rolling gently down to London like an enormous park, it is quite beautiful enough in itself. I never drive through it without a sense of extreme restfulness. All across it the hedge and elm and grass chequer-work is seen at its best: simple, undesigned, and yet somehow designed for permanence. There is nothing except the new arterial roads to disturb its placid continuance from Essex to the Chilterns. It does not suffer from the sudden upheaval which a river of any size gives to a piece of land; it is reputed to be one of the coldest places in England, but I have never seen any proof of it. The essence of its character is its green, friendly tranquillity. No foreigner, anxious to confirm any ideas that England is a sort of enlarged park, would need to go any farther out of London than this. It is the English hedgerow countryside at its undisturbed and dignified best.

South of the Thames all the countryside, plain and hill, weald and woodland, undergoes vast changes. There are northerners who call it too beautiful; we have visitors who cannot keep awake in the strong, soft air coming up from Romney Marsh and the Weald, and who, on waking, eat vastly. The south country is undoubtedly rich and good; its springs are earlier, its autumns push their full fat bellies into the face of winter and knock it almost into the lap of spring. Its variations of landscape in a short space are enormous. They have filled books. But only the Weald, I think, has any place here.

The Weald, once entirely forest, is only partly a plain. But where it is a plain it shares with the Fens the inverted distinction of being one of the unhealthiest spots in England. The thin, sallow Kentish faces indicate the consumptive price paid for the privilege of being born and reared in some of England's most beautiful villages. The land is extremely low; in winter the fat clay is a pudding of stodge that pulls the guts out of a man; in summer it turns into a land of concrete. It floods easily; it is a common sight to see hop gardens standing like the graveyards of derelict ships. If you enquire about houses in the Weald the house agent feels forced to remind you, in apology, " of course its down on the Weald." There is a feeling of oppression

87

that the black rich land of the Fens never gives; the Fens have a mysterious, uplifting air of width and a sort of spacious desolation. They impress; the Weald depresses. Yet the Weald enjoys an immense reputation for beauty.

This beauty again springs almost entirely from the pattern drawn by man on the original flat canvas of the land. Here, as in the whole length of the limestone ridge from Somerset to Rutland, the natural materials for building could not have been better. The forest provided the wood, the land the bricks. The result is one of the most glorious combinations of architectural material that England can show: the multi-coloured, winey-blue Wealden bricks and the massive age-blanched timbers that show up in the house fronts like the skeletons of wooden ships. The Weald is full of such houses, and even of villages comprised almost entirely of such houses: Smarden, Biddenden, Benenden, Frittenden, Rolvenden, Goudhurst, Sissinghurst, Cranbrook, Appledore. They are perfect examples, Biddenden and Benenden almost too perfect, of the English show village. They light up the land with their patterns of dark timber and white plaster as effectively as the colour-washed houses light up the Midland plain. Yet they belong to a world that continually seems to me entirely different. It is the creation of a world of yeomen farmers. Its chief architectural glories are its huge farmhouses, with their sky triangles of oasts. The great country mansion, seen at its most perfect in Midland houses like Drayton and Burghley and Kirby Hall, has scarcely any place here; the sublime, heavenly spired churches of the Northamptonshire lowlands are cathedrals in comparison with the squat, square-towered churches of the Kent and Sussex plain. After a lifetime of craning my neck at spires I can hardly lower myself to look at these humble little places. Mr G. M. Young, in an essay on the English country house, has remarked that the Domesday landscape "reached its high point of pride and beauty in the middle of the nineteenth century; and its mid-point everywhere in the country house." This is right; but it is worth noting that of the illustrations which adorn his essay only one is of a house in the south country, and there is no doubt that the entire scheme of domestic and ecclesiastical architecture is less impressive here than in the Midlands, the north and the near west. I will not attempt any explanation of that fact here, though the Weald of a hundred years ago, seen through the eyes of Cobbett, must supply part of the answer. In winter this morass of land, impassable even for judges on circuit, its roads axle-deep in mud, was nothing but an enormous chilly pudding of sour and unhealthy clay. At the same time the plain of Northamptonshire and Rutland had reached the height of its fashion as a country retreat. One glance at Stamford, with buildings as noble as many in Bath and its six remaining churches, all that are left of twice as many, is enough to show how elegant and complete that fashion was. The Weald can produce nothing like it. It is a world composed of farmers as opposed to landed gentry, a world uninfluenced by an aristocracy which, however false and corrupt and despicable in other respects, knew the secret of building the most magnificent houses that England has ever seen.

But though the two plains are so entirely different in many ways and each poorer for lacking something which the other possesses abundantly—oast-houses and stone mansions are only two examples of it—they are alike in one thing. They are built and bound together by the same fundamental pattern: the pattern of hedge and tree and pasture. It is true that in the south country the hedges have entirely changed in character, that elm and ash have also given way to a predominance of oak and beech, and that the pastures seem less wide and rolling, but the sum of both is worked out over the same common denominator. And of all three it is the hedge, I think, which is most truly English. Other countries can produce fields, a wealth of trees beside which our own appear often very ordinary. But no other country can produce anything which, like stitchery, binds together the varying pattern of the landscape in such a way that the pattern is made infinitely more beautiful.

If this seems extravagant, try to consider the English landscape without the hedge. It would not be the English landscape. The abolition of the common field system no doubt robbed the poor, a century or so ago, of many dearly held privileges; but in the quick hedge it bestowed a common glory on all of us. Though it goes against all my principles to say so, it was not the first time that a score for the great landowners was also a means of beautifying the English landscape. In fact, I doubt if the poor have ever beautified the English landscape. It is the rich and prosperous who have left on it the hall-marks of beauty: the great parks, the woods, the magnificent country mansions, the castles, the New Forest, the beautiful southern farmhouses, towns like Bath and Stamford, villages like Long Melford and Burford. In the same way the Enclosure Acts, benefiting the rich, bestowed on us the most beautiful common inheritance, next to grass, that the English possess. Without the hedge we should all be poorer. I was brought up in a district notable for its lack of trees, but which should have been famous, as I now know, for its magnificent hedges. Without those hedges, huge lines of hawthorn umbrellas, making shade for cattle, that countryside would have been unbearably dull. Nothing

89

else could have made it so beautiful in may-time, when the cream of the hawthorn bloom rose on the four sides of every field, making the air over-faint with scent. Nothing else could have created so happily the first rich drowsy feeling of summer.

In the south I have become acquainted with an entirely different hedge. In the Midlands the commonest hedge is undoubtedly the plain straight-set quick. Time has embroidered it with wild rose and blackberry, occasional ash seedlings, bits of maple, but the quick remains indomitable. In the south, hedges are far more varied; quick is merely one colour, and no longer the common colour, in the pattern. If I walk out of my house I come straightway on a hedge which reads like a catalogue of shrubs: holly, dwarf oak, elder, maple, willow, wild cherry, spindle, hazel, wild rose, sallow, honeysuckle, blackberry, wild clematis, blackthorn, and, always binding it together, hawthorn. Along other lanes I shall see other variations: ash, sweet chestnut, viburnum, dog-wood, crab apple, alder. There is scarcely any end to the variations of the south-country hedge. This means that it is a thing of constant fascination throughout the twelve months of the year: in winter the comforting polished clumps of holly and their scarlet berries and the toy wooden balls of oak apples; in very early spring the catkins of hazel and sallow, the mouse-ear leaves of honeysuckle and elder; in spring the catkins of alder, the white stars of blackthorn, the emerald bread-and-cheese of hawthorn itself; in late spring the little odd trembling bouquets of wild cherry on coppery new leaves, the hawthorn bloom; in summer the glory of wild rose and elder bloom and honeysuckle; in autumn black and scarlet berries, nuts, the slit cerise-and-orange spindle seeds, old man's beard, acorns, the first bare dog-wood branches, the shining, comforting holly again.

But this is not all. This is only what the hedge is. It takes no account of what lives in or under it, or what flowers it shelters. In the Midlands we never expected a hedge to yield more than a patch of violets, a run of celandines, some pinky wild geraniums, late summer riots of willow-herb in damp places. In the south every roadside hedge is a spring glory of primrose and bluebell, white anemones and violets, clouds of lady-smocks and campion; a summer tangle of fox-glove and meadowsweet, wild Canterbury bell and bay willow-herb, a hunting place for wild strawberries. The hedge, beginning as a simple device for the division of the land, has become the haven sheltering every sort of flower and weed that pasturing and the plough drive out. Taken for twelve months of the year, in fact, the southern hedgerow is the most constant of all sources of satisfaction in the landscape. Yet even it, I think, reaches its glory at the flowering season of its commonest flower. When the kex is in bloom the hedge is etherealised. The light dense cloud of creamy flower lace, smothering the hedge itself, lifs it from earth. I cannot remember any writer pausing to pay proper tribute to the kex, humblest of all flowers, rabbit-feed when young, make-believe lace in the games of little girls when in blossom, superb material for the whistles and pea shooters of small boys at the height of summer. It is one of the things, like the hedge itself, which we take for granted. Yet I never see it now without marvelling at its effect of lace-light foam. It is something whipped airily out of the milk of spring.

But flowers are only a moderate part of the life of a hedge. Its position as a sanctuary for small birds and animals is unique, and the records of English small bird life would be poorer if it were not for the hedge. This is not the place to begin a disquisition on bird life, but the springs of most of us would be poorer if there had never been such a thing as a bird's nest in a hedge. The moment of crushing up against the hedge, the thorns pricking the body, the groping forward with one hand, the last stretch of fingers to the nest, the moment of touching eggs, the cold shock of touching raw, featherless young birds: these are all things which the hedgerow, more than anything else, has allowed us to experience infinitely. I see my own children, even at the age of four or five, reach out for this experience of nest-hunting in hedges more eagerly than for any other experience in the countryside, and I find it satisfying to think that in adult life it will be the hedge that provides them with one of the richest of childhood memories.

The southern countryside produces one other type of hedge that is not seen elsewhere. It is the colossal specially trained and pruned hedge of hop gardens, comprised generally of thorns and trained to reach the height of, and make a screen for, the hops themselves. These enormous slices of hedges reach a height of ten, fifteen, or even twenty feet. They are unique to the hop-growing countryside, form the only example of a hedge trained to protect a specific crop. In fact there is now a cult of hedge-cutting, in Midland districts especially, which virtually means the removal of the hedge from arable land. Hedges are hacked so low in order, apparently, to give crops more air and light, that they have ceased to be any protection against wind and cattle at all. A well-laid hedge, like a well-cut ditch, is rapidly becoming a rarity in the countryside—to the complete detriment, as I see it, of the nature and character of the land. Well and properly laid, a hedge is just as beautiful as when in full growth, a supremely satisfying thing to mind and eye. Good hedges and good drainage are, in fact, two of the fundamental necessities of a good agricultural system, yet both, drainage especially, are now often painfully neglected. Before the war the two jobs, like thatching, bred real craftsmen, men of special ability, true to a tradition. The land is poorer for the loss of these men, who were a natural part of a prosperous system.

For, as I see it, the real beauty of the English countryside depends almost entirely on the vigour and prosperity of the agricultural system behind it. This is obviously not true of places of particular natural beauty like Dartmoor or the moors and mountains of Cumberland, Yorkshire, Wales, Derbyshire and so on; but it is undeniably true, and most true, of the type of country with which this essay is specifically dealing. The pudding countryside, unspectacular, quiet, homely, derives its beauty almost solely from the care and order with which it is governed and worked. Like a garden, which begins to be hideous as soon as neglected, it depends almost exclusively on the activities of man for its charm. Grass can be properly green only when properly grazed or cut; arable becomes a wilderness of thistle and dock as soon as plough and seed are withheld from it. If ever the English agricultural system should collapse—and at fairly regular intervals there are signs of its doing so, though it never does—the humble green pudding countryside would be the first to suffer and go into decay with it. We make a great struggle, and rightly so, to preserve acres of downland and moor and woodland and forest from the dangers of so-called progress. We rightly estimate that it would be a catastrophe if the English countryside were bit by bit robbed of such natural features. But if the day ever comes when the English farmer can no longer afford to grow oats and barley, wheat and potatoes, to lay fields for hay, to graze cattle and herd sheep, then we shall be faced with a still deeper catastrophe and the loss of a kind of beauty which we take as naturally for granted as the air we breathe.

Perhaps we take it too much for granted. Consider the English landscape without moor and fell, downland and mountain, and then try to consider it without this plain, pasture-and-arable pudding which is a common part, almost, of its every county. Consider it without fields of wheat, pink-bellied oats, grey-mauve sweet stretches of beans in flower, yellow splashes of mustard, white seas of barley, fields of white peas, blue flax, hops, lucerne, roots, sanfoin, potatoes in flower: all the established crops of the English landscape. Consider it finally without grass and hedgerow, the common and constant elements which bind the whole pattern together. Consider for a single moment an English landscape deprived of these simple and accepted things. And then ask yourself how easily you could give them up.

X

O More than Happy Countryman

RURAL problems, more especially those of rural regeneration, tend to become regarded as rural problems exclusively, as though town life and country life were two unassociated existences. The consequent attitude, which often seems to argue that the town is trying to take something away from the country or alternatively to deny it something, is to my mind mistaken. The problems of the countryside are not, and can hardly ever be in a small country like England, exclusive to the countryside. Nor can country life exist in an hermetically sealed compartment. Country life and town life are interlocked, complementary, and until this is realised much hopeful talk about post-war rural regeneration will, I think, have no point at all.

For example, I was recently asked, with several other authors, to express my views on rural education in a periodical famous for its sound approach to all rural problems. My reply was that the best rural education in the world had little point until it ceased to be accompanied by low standards of diet and home-life, and that I had noted from careful observation that physical debility in country children often disappeared as soon as they attended a town school where one good cooked meal a day was provided. I gave as my conclusion that what was important was not what happened at school but what happened, or did not happen, at home. The replies of some other authors astonished me. They took the view that the part played in modern civilisation by country and town were naturally conflicting, roughly those of angel and devil, that the pure character of one was being consistently defiled by the malignant influences of the other, and that nothing would be right again until country people were made to realise that country life, if it were to survive at all, must be entirely separated and set free from town culture, town influences and town education. One author even went so far as to declare: " I should like to tear down the pictures of city scenes and objects which defile the classroom walls even of schools in the Outer Hebrides."

This is one example of what might be called the compartmental attitude. Take another: the editor of a paper dealing with rural life was mournfully telling me how he had invited a famous novelist to write a descriptive article about a certain part of England. When the article arrived he was pained to discover that she had shut herself up in an oyster shell. She had resolutely refused to describe a single beautiful feature of landscape, simply because she was afraid if she did so that hundreds of less fortunate townspeople might be tempted to discover her pet beauty spots for themselves. Her attitude was that all townspeople are philistines and that the countryside and its beauty must be jealously guarded against them. It evidently did not occur to her that many of the devoutest lovers of the countryside, many of those most anxious for its future and the preservation of its beauties, are people forced by jobs and circumstances to spend most of their lives in cities and towns. Nor did it occur to her that many of those most ignorant of country life, most insensitive and careless of its future and proper government, are those who are forced for some reason or other to live entirely in the country.

The first of these authors apparently wants to deny country children even the simple right of comparing country life with a picture of town or city; in short, though a man of wide cultural horizons himself, he wants to shorten the horizon of the country child so that it will never hanker after life beyond the nearest hedge. The second wants to deny the townsman the simple right of looking at the beauty of the country-side, though there is no indication that she expects the townsman, in return, to deny her the beauties (cathedrals, churches, old buildings, squares, good streets, theatres, and so on) of the town. She belongs to the school, which if anything seems to increase, that regards the countryside as a preserve, but simply thinks of the town as a public playground. In short, though both authors would resent, and quite rightly resent, any interference with their own choice of cultural contacts, they are very ready to impose exactly that limitation on someone else.

These attitudes to my mind are very wrong. There emerges a third, which seems to regard the salvation of the countryside as dependent on the production of good agriculturists, honest craftsmen, and in general of sound workers in some way connected with the soil. To this school the rural worker is necessarily and inevitably an agricultural worker. As such his place, and those of his fellow countrymen, is on the land.

But the fact is that there are forty kinds, and not one kind, of rural worker. Their occupations are often identical with those of town workers, and every village contains examples of them. The village I always have in mind lies in a pastoral county of orchards, woods and hop gardens under the Kentish Downs; it is in the heart of one of the most fruitful agricultural districts of England. Yet of its two hundred and fifty inhabitants quite a small proportion only are agricultural workers. Since people must have letters, coal, electric light, bread, furniture and linen, there are also postmen, coal-men, electricians, bakers, upholsterers, flax workers; there is a machine tool engineer, a chauffeur, a garage mechanic, a horse trainer, a carpenter, an insurance agent, an optician; there are paper workers, estate agents, quarrymen, brick-workers, bricklayers, caretakers, bus drivers; and since railways run through the country, and villages have stations, there are also a number of railway workers. Yet all these men, though their trades are unconnected with the soil and are part of that mechanical life which rural reformers often view with such horror, are country workers. They live in the country, though some may work in the town; their children are educated in the country; their instincts lie there. And though they have nothing to do with the beautiful traditional crafts of the countryside—such as ploughing, reaping, threshing, lambing, which photograph so well—they are an essential part of its life. Indeed they may be said to be a more essential part of its life than the ploughman, the reaper or the shepherd, whose products are produced out of the country but not exclusively for it, whose harvest of bread and potatoes and fruit and meat is produced to feed town homes.

To attempt to segregate these workers, shutting them carefully up in a compartment governed by separate rules, is nonsense. To deny their children the right to at least some chance of the widest educational contacts on the ground that country children should be country educated is reactionary as well as absurd. A census of the leading men of the day, from politicians to engineers, from executives to editors, would reveal a surprising number of men born in rural homes. For these men the cultural centres of life, the material sources by which their education was developed, were not the Outer Hebrides. The semi-monastic life of island seclusion is only for the few, and those few are unwise to attempt to impose its restricted delights on others simply because what is right for them must be right for other people.

It is therefore my view that town life, hideous though it may be to the most sensitive, appalling in architecture, monstrous in its unchecked development, is inextricably bound up with country life, and that in any sound post-war reconstruction this will have to be taken into account. Certain principles of town life, such as education, may have to be reshaped so that they may serve both town and country. For example, the rural education system is already partially a town system. Smaller country schools (often insanitary, yet capable of renovation) have been closed and younger children are now conveyed to central villages by chartered bus or taxi. This works quite well. Older children attend centralised town schools—often with excellent physical results. In the post-war reconstruction, in which there must inevitably be vast rebuilding of town schools, it would be an admirable thing if the new schools could be built beyond the limits of the town and from there serve both town and the adjacent rural district. To these new schools, town-planned but built in the country, could go all country children from five upwards. The small rural schools, reconditioned, could become nursery schools for children of from two to five, thereby solving the rural mother's greatest problem. For the rural mother, who is often forced to go out to work for at least some part of the day, is at present denied the right given to so many mothers in town and city: the admirable and necessary right of the nursery school. In this way both younger and older children could be ensured of at least one soundly cooked meal a day—a thing which, through ignorance, laziness or sheer economic impossibility, many of them now never get.

Economic impossibility: the nicer expression. Bad wages: the simpler. For sooner or later any plan of rural reconstruction will have to take into account the plain, unpleasant and cynical fact that the rural worker, fed on fancy phrases like " extended facilities for the teaching of local crafts," etc., is still poorly paid. Whenever country wages are discussed it is customary to point to the agricultural worker. But the low standard is general. Country postmen, whose winter journeys are often feats of heroism, are shockingly paid, and in the village I have already mentioned there are three railway workers who, out of the absolute necessity to turn existence into something slightly better, put in from ten to fifteen hours' extra work, evenings and week-ends, in the gardens of those better off than themselves. Another postman makes ends meet by running a cobbler's shop. The average wage for working gardeners is between two pounds and fifty shillings; that for council road workers about forty-five shillings; that for lorry drivers, working fantastic hours sometimes on the Covent Garden fruit runs, about three pounds. To these amounts, now taxed, the average country worker, or his wife, is bound to do something to contribute a supplement.

It is generally argued, however, that if wages are low in the country, rents and goods are correspondingly low. Is this true? I will take half a dozen typical cottages in this Kentish village, which owing to the war lacks its long-promised council houses. First a bungalow: four rooms, bath, decent garden, wooden shed, leaking roof, damp walls, bad drainage, rent nineteen-and-six a week; another bungalow: three rooms, no bath, damp walls, fair sanitation, decent garden, rent twelve-and-six a week; a cottage: four rooms, earth privy, damp walls, fair garden, no bath, bad kitchen, rent ten shillings a week; three other cottages: amenities much the same as the last, rent ten shillings. These rents are out of all proportion to the amenities provided. The day of the half-crown cottage has gone. On some estates there are still workers' cottages at five shillings; there is still free milk and sometimes free firewood on the best-run farms. But these end those privileges of the country worker which are popularly supposed to compensate him for low wages.

He is in fact faced with unexpected expenses. The village shop, which must of course carry an absurd bazaar variation of stock from carrot-seed to corsets, from biscuits to buckets, from cretonne to chillies, is apt to charge the outside farthing. It enjoys a monopoly. The only way to challenge this monopoly is to shop in the nearest town: fare one shilling by bus. The shilling probably represents all, perhaps more than, the saving on the town-bought goods. An alternative is the local carrier, who, in an ancient Ford, will bring out anything from a packet of peas to a mangle, charging from twopence upwards as carriage. All this, in however small a way, adds to the living expenses of the country worker. For he can live in the country, but not on it. He can grow his own fruit and vegetables, but his meat, bread, newspapers, groceries, fish, coal, and many other things must come out to him from a larger village or town. For the privilege of having his newspaper delivered he pays an extra penny a week. He is in fact so dependent on outside supplies that this often induces in his suppliers a corresponding feeling of independence. Sometimes the fish-man calls; sometimes not. And those who neglect to buy their coal on Saturdays will be lucky if they get another delivery within a week.

The countryside is, therefore, less self-supporting than any other section of the community. It is true that it produces wheat, potatoes, cattle, fruit, milk, wood, but it does not produce coal, shoes, cloth, tea, tools, pottery, hats, furniture, linen and so on. These are the products of the despised town, on which the countryman is for ever invited to turn his back. The return to country crafts is an excellent motto, but it is fantastic to suppose that the countryside could exist on handicrafts, however excellent, and still more fantastic to suppose that the vastly increased population of England since the Industrial Revolution could be supplied by goods produced by the loving and laborious skill of the hands.

I think we must face this. The production of country woollens, iron and forged steel work, baskets, pleasant pottery, woodwork and so on, charming though it may be, offers no solution to the economic survival of the countryside. It is a process of going back, of seeking a remedy for the future out of the past. It is rather as if agriculturists were to advocate the use of oxen in order to replace the tractor. The picturesque, though it may also be useful, is not enough. The Great War of 1914-18 delivered a final blow of disintegration to a type of rural life which in many respects had not changed for a hundred, in some ways for two hundred, years. Whether it wrought changes for good or evil is momentarily not of importance. The disruptive, revolutionary nature of the change itself is enough. Church, squire-archy, agriculture, class distinctions were all struck, split, changed, devitalised as influences. The trinity of parson-squire-farmer was broken. The countryside, opened up by new means of communication, ceased to be a remote and separate unit. It became inevitably linked with and dependent on the town.

Ever since that time we have had reformers who deplored the passing of a quieter and apparently more satisfied country life, in which ploughmen were content to be ploughmen, in which work was done by the strength of horses and the hands of man. These reformers have advocated that we should turn back, reapply the methods of the past, and solve our problems by all getting together in a good old-fashioned, honest and merry way round the parish pump. All the time, as so often happens, the changing shape of country life has been dictated by other things. For the most unmistakable change in the countryside of the last quarter of a century is that it has become the dormitory, the living-space of the town. And within the last year it has become something more: the refuge, the very life-space of the stricken population of the town.

These two facts are significant. It is not many years since Bernard Shaw (who now lives in a village) wrote a scathing castigation of the dark, muddy, boring life of the countryside. Today it is town and city that are insufferable, both in peace and war, since bombing is only a terrifyingly aggravated version of the normal nerve-racket of town life. The town worker, rushing to catch his bus, tube or tram, eating hastily in crowded restaurants, crossing streets with his life in his hands, inevitably seeks an antidote to the strain imposed by these things. He becomes, as soon as economically possible, not simply a town worker, but a town worker with a country home. His proudest boast is " a cottage in the country."

All this has inevitably affected country life. Not in the entire history of the English people have so many people been conscious of the countryside as they are today. There was never a time when so many books and articles were demanded, and written, on that subject. This in itself is an excellent thing. That there should be a demand, long before the war has ended, for a plan of reconstructed post-war rural life is a highly significant thing. Even if serious rural reformers are still comparatively few, it is clear that by the end of the war a vast new mass of the population will be country-conscious and probably country-loving. The man who begins by using the country as a dormitory soon begins to use it for week-ends, holidays and odd days, thus spending more than half his life there. The family who is bombed out of its city home into the country may never return to the city to make another. Our so-called civilisation has, in fact, produced a hybrid, a town-countryman, whose existence and vital needs it is impossible to ignore.

For soon these week-enders, dormitory-workers, bombed-out families become part of country life, paying country taxes, dependent on country government, supplies, administration. They are not rural workers but rural dwellers. Their immediate influence on country life is to effect improvements on cottages and gardens, and to raise, by example, the standard of living. Their children will attend, perhaps, the village school, where pinafores and serge dresses used to be the rule. But the newcomers wear gym dresses, and soon half the girls in the school are wearing gym dresses. Similarly, it used to be jam sandwiches, perhaps bread and marge, packed for the school midday meal; but now the newcomers bring sandwiches with various fillings, cold meat pies, fruit jellies, thermos flasks of hot soup, and soon the child with the jam sandwiches is naturally demanding these things. The new country dweller is thus, through a higher economic standard, bringing a new influence, a new example and a new problem to the country. For out of a wage of fifty shillings or so it is hard to provide daily meat pies and little jellied luxuries; it is hard, perhaps impossible, to reach that higher standard.

So finally it all comes back to a problem of money. The notion that the country worker, because he enjoys free fresh air, pleasant scenery, fresh vegetables and the songs of birds, must be content with a correspondingly lower wage than the town worker, is in need of radical change. The further notion that the countryside itself is entertainment enough and that the countryman does not need the relaxation of cinema, Woolworths or an occasional shop-window fuddle, is pernicious. The countryman can no longer be tied to the parish pump and the maypole; the straw-chewing yokel is dead; today his counterpart hops a bus, plays the slot machines, finds solace in Ginger Rogers, and has a cup of tea at a sandwich bar in a chain store. Useless to say that this is a sad thing and a decadent thing, and that we must turn the countryman back to the straight and narrow path of honest toil, barn dances and content. If the countryman prefers other things, what can we do? If we aim to create happier countrymen, and these things make countrymen happier, what right have we to deny them?

But higher wages, so desirable if the country worker proper is to be kept on the land, at once open up the huge and terrifying problem of agricultural policy, with all its muddle and controversy. On the one side the labourer can point to the iniquitous situation whereby he is told that he represents the largest community of workers in the country, the most essential in time of war, and yet still receives a comparatively low wage and is the last of all sections of workers to receive the privilege of insurance benefit. " If I am so important," he may well say, " am I not entitled to be paid better? Munition workers earn ten or more pounds a week. Yet the food I produce is more important than fish and even, I am told, more important than guns."

The other side of the argument is equally familiar. The farmer points to tithes, high rents, the appalling costs of feeding stuffs, the necessity for expensive machinery (as in dairy work), the uncertainties of weather and markets, the restrictions on this and that. " Mine is a twenty-four-hour-a-day job," he may say, " and the work of a whole summer may be ruined by a thunderstorm or by a sudden importation of barley from the Baltic. I am at the mercy of fuddling politicians, who when pressed finally declare that agriculture itself is at the mercy of foreign investments. Higher wages would ruin me."

All true; yet it never seems to occur to farmers, at election time, to

The straw-chewing yokel is dead.

cast a vote in the opposite of their traditional direction. The infamous Kettering speech, in which farmers were told the plain painful truth that they must expect to be sacrificed on the altar of foreign invest-ments, was an excellent example of the farmer being strangled by those he had put into power. Nor does it seem to occur to farmers that, if only they would combine with their own workers, they represent a most powerful force for the manipulation of improved agricultural conditions for all. This powerful combination of farmer and worker could produce some hasty changes at Westminster, but the distrust and insularity of farmers, as a class generally, is exceedingly hard to break down. They are a remarkable class, I notice, for the passing of resolutions; but the setting up of a powerful common front with their own workers against the common forces of cynical exploitation is apparently too revolutionary a thing for them to consider. Yet all agricultural revolutions must, as Sir George Stapledon has pointed out, " spring from the land itself, and that is to say from the farmers them-selves," and we shall get nearer a revolution in farming when, at last, farmers themselves can make up their minds, collectively, that that is true not only of themselves but of the men who work their land.

From these remarks the impression may perhaps have been gathered that I regard the country worker, whether he is labourer or postman, gardener or railway man, as an innocent wage slave having a raw deal, and that the sole villains in the piece are the farmers, landowners, hop merchants, corn merchants and railway directors. It is true that I would like to see the country worker better paid and that I think he must be better paid if the drift from the land is, in post-war days, to be stopped. But the countryman is far from being without faults. What of the countryman's efforts to help rural progress? to protect his privileges? to promote better citizenship? After ten years of intimate observation, five of participation in parish government, my conclusion is that the average countryman does not care a damn for these things. One of the hardest things to inculcate in him is a sense of social responsibility. He cares more about gossip than progress, rates the pint higher than the privilege of voting his own rural parliament, and only becomes aware of rights when they are being or have been taken away from him. The average public attendance at the meetings of the parish council of which I am chairman is, for example, one per meeting. Often that one is a person who wishes to air, year in, year out, the same grievances. Yet at these meetings the construction of council houses, education, light, water, common land, dangerous corners, rates, and the general spending of what is always ominously called " other people's money " are discussed. All are treated with a fathomless indifference.

This indifference spreads through the whole community, rich and poor, leisured and labouring alike. I notice it breaks, however, when there is any likelihood of a public beanfeast or when the parson, after a delay for consultation with the parish council, neglects to distribute the few paltry shillings of an ecclesiastical charity dead on the appointed day.

It seems to me useless, therefore, to talk of higher wages and attendant emancipation until this indifference is broken, until the countryman is made to realise that rural progress is in his own hands and is not something that is going to be gratuitously conferred on him like a medal from outside. The countryman is notoriously suspicious of outside influence, yet he has only his own apathy to blame if a misguided outsider decides to run, and ruin, his parish affairs. Such apathy has already cost my own village a plantation of rare trees, chopped down by an enlightened outsider, and a financial debt which will shackle us for years. Perhaps the countryman generally, like the farmer particularly, is too suspicious of or too insusceptible to change. Although in a quarter of a century the countryside has changed more radically than it previously changed in two hundred years, yet in some ways the countryman himself remains unadjusted to the difference. There lingers the notion that parish affairs ought still, for some reason, to be in the hands of the parson, the farmer, the landowner, the retired colonel, the doctor, and that "it's no use going to the parish meeting, anyway, because it's all been cut and dried between chairman and clerk beforehand."

One is sometimes forced, therefore, towards the conclusion that the countryman does not want to be helped or to help himself, and that so long as things go tolerably well he will be content with the old sweet way. One meets continually with appalling ignorance, no less appalling lack of responsibility. Gossip, with all its pettiness, its curdling and embittering effect, still takes precedence over progress in the scale of rural values. The case of the village that wanted a younger parson is interesting. For years it had complained, with truth, that its parson was too old, too autocratic, too out of touch. "Give us," the people said, "a young man, with a young wife, who will liven things up." The young parson and the young wife finally arrived. With what results? An embittered outbreak of personal resentment, backbiting, spy-mania, class prejudice and downright hostility. The young parson, in despair, finds his faith severely shattered: for these demonstrations came not from outside the church but from within it. Young, virile, enlightened, friendly, capable of a most broad-minded view on any subject from beer to abortion, this bewildered clergyman is forced at last to confess that his only friends are those who never set foot inside his church.

It is hard to keep faith polished up in these circumstances. Harder still with the knowledge that, after the war, the church itself will be closed, the living joined with another. The church, too, like the big house and the parish council, is near to becoming a spent force. The self-contained, perhaps self-satisfied, shell of village life as it used to be is broken. Will it be restored? Do we want it restored? I think all who hope for its restoration on the lines of the past, on a utopian system where the motto is " The country for country folk !" are living in a reactionary dream. Country life is, as I have tried to show in these pages, the best life in the world. To regard it as an air-tight compartment reserved only for the few is to invite its decay, and though it is against all the principles of solemn rural reformers to say that it must become more and more allied with, and not separate from, the town, this is my view. Like night and day, male and female, summer and winter, the town and the country are complementary forces and pleasures in man's existence. The revolution of 1914-18 brought them closer together than ever before; the revolution of 1942 will bring them closer still. " O more than happy countryman," said Virgil, " if only he knew his good fortune." But O still more happy countryman who is big enough to understand, enlarge, improve, protect and share that good fortune with others.

COUNTRY CLASSICS

This popular series of quality paperbacks includes famous classics and forgotten masterpieces of writing about the countryside and rural subjects. The books are all produced in a 216 x 135mm format with beautiful colour covers. Selected titles are available in hardback.

Adventures Among Birds
W. H. Hudson

W. H. Hudson was one of the great field naturalists and ornithologists of the last century. In this book, he describes incidents and adventures watching birds across England, from wild geese in Norfolk to goldfinches in Dorset.

'This enchanting book is about the time before motorways and about the pure joy of having ears and eyes.'

EDWARD BLISHON,
Pick of the Paperbacks,
Radio 4

Paperback £3.95
Hardback £8.95

Country Tales
H. E. Bates

The best of H. E. Bates's much-loved stories about the countryside gathered together in one volume. The book contains 25 tales set in the remote hamlets, villages and market towns of England in the 1910s, 20s and 30s.

Every story is available only in this edition, which includes such classics as 'The Black Boxer', 'The Woman Who Had Imagination' and 'Harvest Moon'.

£4.95

Paperback only

The Country House-Wife's Garden
William Lawson

The first book ever written on gardening for women, a delightful pot-pourri of hints and gardening lore written in the seventeenth century by a Yorkshire parson. A perfect gift for the gardener.

Introduced by Rosemary Verey.

'This is an enchanting book.'

ALAN MELVILLE, Popular Gardening

Paperback £2.50
Hardback £4.95

The Essential Gilbert White of Selborne

The first popular selection from all of White's writings. A perfect introduction for the newcomer to White and Selborne.

Illustrated with wood engravings by Eric Ravilious.

Paperback £4.95
Hardback £8.95
384pp

Gypsy Folk Tales
John Sampson (Ed.)

Nothing brings us closer to the spirit of Romany life than these strange, haunting tales of poor country folk, beggars and travellers in a land of giants and dragons, great mansions, hovels, enchanted castles, witchcraft and magic.

'His great collections of folk-tales are treasure-houses of quaint expressions and beautiful turns of phrase.'

WALTER STARKIE

Paperback only £3.50

Life in a Devon Village
Henry Williamson

An enchanting memoir of village life in the Twenties. A companion volume to *Village Tales*.

'A welcome reprint ... Williamson is still our best nature writer since Richard Jefferies.'

BRIAN JACKMAN, The Sunday Times

Paperback £3.95
Hardback £8.95

Memoirs of a Surrey Labourer
George Bourne

'There's writing for you.'　　　　　HENRY WILLIAMSON

Paperback only £4.95

The Old Farm
Thomas Hennell

A fascinating record of traditional farms and farming methods, it presents a vivid portrait of old-fashioned country life and lore, from the dialects of the shepherds to cider-making, straw-plaiting and charcoal-burning, from weather-forecasting to mole-catching.

Paperback only £3.95

Sweet Thames Run Softly
Robert Gibbings

The story of a summer journey by rowing boat from the source of the Thames to London. Illustrated throughout with the author's own wood engravings.

'For the soul's refreshment read and keep this book. It is wise, kindly and full of lovely things.'

Sunday Times

'An intoxicating book, almost Edwardian in spirit.'
ANDREW LANGLEY, Daily Telegraph

'An enchanting experience ... there is only one other in the compendium of Thames literature which is deserving of inclusion in the same class — the immortal Three Men in a Boat.'

SENEX, Oxford Times

Paperback only £3.95

ORDER FORM

COUNTRY CLASSICS

		Hardback	Paperback
—	ADVENTURES AMONG BIRDS	£8.95	£3.95
—	THE COUNTRY HOUSE-WIFE'S GARDEN		£2.50
—	COUNTRY TALES	—	£4.95
—	THE ESSENTIAL GILBERT WHITE	£8.95	£4.95
—	GYPSY FOLK TALES	—	£3.50
—	LIFE IN A DEVON VILLAGE	£8.95	£3.95
—	MEMOIRS OF A SURREY LABOURER	—	£4.95
—	THE OLD FARM	—	£3.95
—	SWEET THAMES RUN SOFTLY	—	£3.95

If you cannot find these titles in your bookshop, they can be obtained directly from the publisher. Indicate the number of copies required and fill in the form below (in block letters please):

NAME ....

ADDRESS ....

....

....

Send to Robinson Publishing Cash Sales, P.O. Box 11, Falmouth, Cornwall TR10 9EN. Please enclose cheque or postal order to the value of the cover price plus: In UK only – 55p for the first book, 22p for the second book, and 14p for each additional book to a maximum £1.75. BFPO and Eire – 55p for the first book, 22p for the second book, and 14p for the next seven books and 8p for each book thereafter. Overseas – £1.25 for the first book, 31p per copy for each additional book.

Whilst every effort is made to keep prices low, it is sometimes necessary to increase prices at short notice. Robinson Publishing reserve the right to show on covers, and charge, new retail prices which may differ from those advertised in text or elsewhere.